FITZGERALD'S FUNNY SCI-FI SHORTS

PATRICE FITZGERALD

PRAISE FOR PATRICE FITZGERALD

One of the sharpest minds and clearest voices writing today."

Hugh Howey, **New York Times** bestselling author of **WOOL**

"Fitzgerald has an eye for nuance, deftly striking chords that will resonate with readers."

Jason Gurley, bestselling author of **Eleanor**

"Fitzgerald's sharp and evocative prose pulls the reader into her stories."

Rysa Walker, author of Amazon Breakthrough Novel Award Grand Prize Winner **Timebound**

"An amazing voice."

Samuel Peralta, **Wall Street Journal** and **USA Today** bestselling author; series editor for **The Future Chronicles.**

"Her stories are strong, her characters vibrant, and her imagination comes to life for her readers."

Ann Christy, **USA Today** bestselling author of the **Strikers** trilogy

Fitzgerald's Funny Sci-Fi Shorts

includes the following stories

FOREWORD

A Quintessential Voice
by Samuel Peralta

I first met Patrice Fitzgerald in an online writers' support group. At the time, we were all fairly new to speculative fiction, with me newer than all the others. Several of our fellow authors had already written original series, albeit none of us had anything close to the commercial and critical success of Hugh Howey's phenomenal *Wool* series. We had gotten together to share tips of the trade, both in writing and in marketing our work, and we were excited at the potential that books like Howey's had revealed.

If I recall correctly, Patrice had at least two or more novels under her belt, including one written in the world of *Wool*—the well-regarded *Karma of the Silo*. I'd written exactly one short story and was using that as my calling card to try to get my foot in the door, mainly in science fiction anthologies as I didn't have the stamina to write novels.

As a back-up measure just in case no one would deign to publish my stories, I was pitching the group on my own anthology, *The Robot Chronicles*.

I remember trying to convince the group that this was a good thing. I'd organize the whole kaboodle, a dozen or so of us would contribute work (including my supposedly unpublishable story), drafts would be red-penciled by editor David Gatewood, and I'd leverage my corporate marketing background to tackle the dingy side of actually selling the book.

The stories poured in, all slick and professional, dystopian tales of artificial intelligence gone amok, grim-dark works of the robot apocalypse, including my own portentous fable of inhumanity.

And then there was Patrice's story.

"I Dream of PIA" was an astonishing—and hilarious—look at one man's encounter with a unique A.I. in the form of his very own Personal Intelligence Assistant. It's a triumphant Hilaire Belloc meets Isaac Asimov moment, unique, uplifting.

She hit another homerun in my third anthology *The Alien Chronicles*, with "Hanging with Humans," an uproarious look at what happens when an intergalactic gameshow sends one of its contestants to the exotic planet Earth—to experience a prom.

And then, for *The A.I. Chronicles*, she delivered "Piece of Cake," which imagined a questionable utopia whose balance was governed by strict rules—on who to marry, how much to exercise, and, in order to maintain the ideal weight, how much cake you're allowed to eat.

It was what I had come to realize was quintessential Fitzgerald, a Douglas Adams-level *tour-de-force* of semi-seriousness and absolute levity, an amazing voice.

The Marvel Cinematic Universe begins with *Iron Man*, and proceeds through a hero's quest cycle of films introducing the Hulk, Thor, and Captain America. The series deepens in complexity and grows darker with *Thor: The Dark World*, and *Captain America: The Winter Soldier*—and then *whammo!*

You hit the opening strains of Redbone's million-selling gold single "Come and Get Your Love" in the *Guardians of the Galaxy*. It's an uproarious and irreverent mash-up of gee-whiz science fiction and flippant humor, played to a catchy soundtrack.

That's Fitzgerald.

In the often apocalyptic and dystopian worlds of science fiction, she's *Ant-Man, Thor: Ragnarok*, an unexpected shaft of sunshine breaking through the thundercloud.

Many will know Patrice from her other, arguably more notable work. She heads a successful publishing company featuring mystery, romance, fantasy, and nonfiction books.

She's a singer of jazz, opera, Broadway. She's a champion of women authors. She helms the space opera anthology series *Beyond the Stars*, which has grown a tremendous following over the years.

But I will always cherish where, for me, delight began— her stories.

Turn the page. Enjoy.

Samuel Peralta
  Toronto, Canada

Samuel Peralta's fiction has hit the USA Today *and* Wall Street Journal *bestsellers lists and been shortlisted for* Best American Science Fiction & Fantasy. *He's the creator and series editor of the* Future Chronicles *anthologies, which were all #1 bestsellers on* Amazon. *Still active in the high-tech start-up community, he's also an art collector and a producer of independent films, including* Golden Globe *nominee* The Fencer, *and the* Emmy Award-*winning sci-fi film* Real Artists.

WINGMAN

Dating Companions® gives you the peace of mind you crave. Our robotic investigators provide accurate information on potential mates—and in real time. We can make sure you steer clear of individuals with criminal records, scary financial liabilities, or communicable diseases.

Visit a Dating Companions® showroom today... and find a lover tomorrow!

WINGMAN

"So how does it work?" Kayla asked, leaning forward in her chair. "I mean, how does a robot look at a guy and figure out if he would be a good match?"

The salesman laughed. He had perfect hair and dazzling teeth.

"Oh no. Our Dating Companions are much more sophisticated than that." He gave Kayla a smile that was right out of Central Casting. "Basically, your DC acts as your wingman. Or in your case, wingwoman. All you do is bring her along to wherever you're going when you'd like to meet someone. She'll sit and chat with you just like a girl-friend would, until you spot a possible target."

"A target?" Kayla asked, her eyebrows raised. She looked away from the salesman's smiling gaze. "I'm not desperate or anything. I have no trouble finding men. In fact," she laughed, "that's the problem. I find them, I date them, I fall in love with them, and then they turn out to be jerks. Story of my life."

The salesman reached across the wood grained desk, his hand stopping just short of hers. He nodded. "Please. Call me Nick."

Kayla smiled and gave a little giggle. She pushed away the possibility that the salesman himself might be available. "Okay, Nick."

"Kayla, you're just the kind of person we designed our newest line of Dating Companions for. We can help with that problem." He gestured around the showroom at the robots standing lifeless, silently watching. "With one of our DCs, you'll know everything about the guy before you get in too deep. Our latest model—DC 73Luv—can analyze a potential partner's suitability on the spot."

His face broke into that movie star smile again. "In fact, the woman who left as you came in? I don't know if you noticed the big rock she was sporting on her finger... she met a great guy last year with the help of one of our DCs. She's getting married in two months."

"Wow, really?" Kayla looked around at the various models on display. "Show me how they work."

"Okay... So, you're telling me that I can be in a bar checking out a babe and this thing will be able to tell me if she has any dirt in her past?" Theo looked around at the bots on the side of the showroom.

The salesman nodded. "Absolutely. Right on the spot. You'll have access to all her records. Everything from talking smack about her ex online to hover car accidents, financial liability, certain unpleasant diseases you might not want to catch..."

"Wow. That's great stuff, man. My last girlfriend was smoking hot, but she turned out to be such bad news."

"Yup. Exactly the kind of thing we can help you avoid." The salesman raised his chin toward the door. "Did you happen to see the guy who left right before you? He was out with some friends last week and met a girl—a beauty—that he was crazy for. Asked her out to dinner. This was before he came here, of course."

"Yeah?" Theo's eyes were on the array of female robots across the room. "So, what happened?"

"He was falling fast. But he decided to get a little insurance. Came in last Wednesday and got a weekend rental rate on one of our latest releases, the TD 770 you see over there. On the left?" The salesman pointed to a robot with a full beard. "Brought the TD to the restaurant where he was meeting the girl, and his Dating Companion did a quick analysis. Guess what he found out?"

Theo raised an eyebrow. "What?"

"Well, she told him about breaking up with a guy recently, but she hadn't mentioned that they were married and that she took him to the cleaners in the divorce. The ex, poor bastard, had to give her six figures a year to make her go away. And all that was after she totaled his Porsche."

"No kidding." Theo shook his head. He gazed around at the silent robots admiringly. "So, what did your customer do?"

"Well, let's just say he came up with a reason never to see her again pretty fast."

Theo pushed back his chair and walked over to one of the robots. "Okay. I'm ready for the demo."

———————

Kayla pulled open the door and was hit with a blast of hot air and loud music. It was Saturday night and the place was crowded. She could feel the thrum of excitement as the rhythmic pulses rippled across the dance floor.

She turned to her DC. "Stay right beside me, Jen."

The robot nodded. "Of course."

The bar was swarming with people; there was no chance of finding one stool, let alone two. Kayla made her way across the room as fingers of purple, then green, then orange light striped the floor. She spotted space for two on a sofa tucked into a corner and headed there as quickly as possible.

She and Jen slid in behind the table, and the sofa formed itself immediately to their contours. A serving bot came over and asked for their drink orders. As soon as it rolled away, Kayla let her gaze sweep around the room. Loud music and clinking glasses accompanied laughter and the scent of humans on the hunt.

She looked at her DC and nodded toward a man who was talking to a guy beside him. He didn't seem to have a partner. "Jen, that guy, there. What can you tell me about him?"

"Are you indicating the man at the table next to the wall who is wearing a blue shirt?"

"Yes. The one talking to that guy with the perfect hair.

Actually, perfect-hair guy looks like a robot. Don't you think?"

Jen became very still for a moment.

"Dress shirt by Azawi. Originally $210, on sale this season for $142. Pants manufactured by Derringer Brothers. Normally sold for just under $100. Shoes designed by Gretsch, $372."

Kayla's eyes opened wide. "Go on," she said.

"Haircut estimated at $120, probably from Emilio at Zanzibar. The bulge in his left pocket suggests that he's carrying the most recently released device from Apple, $2,099. He appears to be drinking a Dirty Stingball, alcohol content approximately 52%. Height cannot be determined with precise accuracy as he is in a seated position, but I judge him to be between 5'11" and 6 feet. Weight estimated at 172. BMI range 18.5 to 20%. Based on those figures, he could imbibe three such drinks over a two-and-one-half-hour period with no gross motor skill impairment."

Kayla's mouth was open. She closed it.

"What else?"

Jen's eyes stared straight ahead. "Locating photo match now."

A moment passed. Kayla took a sip of her drink.

"Subject has been identified with 99.5% accuracy. Theodore Cleveland. Age 32. Owns a two-bedroom residence in Oaktree Commons. Employed with Richmond Hospital—"

"He's a doctor?"

"He works in the health management department.

Annual salary $187,000 per year with an annual bonus typically equaling 7% of base salary. He drives this year's model hover car made by Benz-Royce. Silver, with wood inserts. Plate number H07DZ9."

Jen stopped and looked at Kayla.

Kayla thought she detected a glow of satisfaction in the robot's mechanical eyes. She shook her head. "That is amazing."

Jen smiled. "Would you like me to access financial records?"

Kayla nodded. "Absolutely."

Jen concentrated. "He has an account at New Athenian bank. Savings of $8,337.02. His credit rating is 879. Stock holdings totaling $237,000, 12% of which comprise shares of the hospital he currently works for. Bank and credit card records show a spending pattern that is within fiscally responsible limits for an individual of his earning capacity and resources."

She turned toward Kayla. "Would you like me to access criminal records?"

Kayla nodded slowly. "He sounds so amazing I'm almost afraid to hear more. It might ruin the picture." She laughed. "But I suppose I should know."

Jen got that faraway look again. "I am reviewing records of any pertinent criminal activity, charges or convictions, and lawsuits. I see nothing other than a traffic ticket from three years previously. Subject received a citation for ignoring a limit on the number of vehicles permitted at a certain altitude in a residential zone."

Kayla sighed. "He sounds perfect. And just look at

him! I think I'm in love." She took another sip of her drink. "I can't believe he's alone. Maybe he just broke up with someone? What an incredible catch for somebody." She smiled at Jen. "Okay, now how do I actually meet him? Do you help with that part too?"

"So, buddy, what are you gonna do with that drink?"

"Oh, I can manage a drink or two. We're designed to be able to interact with humans in a realistic way. I can pour liquid down my throat with the best of them. There's a tank inside for evenings like this."

Theo slapped his companion on the back. "This is gonna be fun." He looked around at the crowded room. "Hey. We need to give you a name. If I have to introduce you to anybody..."

"Yes. I need a name."

"Do you have one? I mean, something you go by when you're on these assignments?"

His companion smiled. "If I did, it wouldn't matter. They wipe our memories after every assignment—or each new client, anyway. Wouldn't want us giving away any secrets."

"Huh." Theo thought for a moment. "Okay. I'm going to call you Rob. Rob for robot."

Rob laughed. "Good one."

Theo turned his attention back to the people around them. He lifted his chin to point toward a girl three tables away. "How about her? Long hair, red dress?"

Rob nodded. "Got it." He closed his eyes for a moment.

"I've matched her with online pictures. Party girl, works in the city. Lots of drinking. Likes a good time."

"Mmm... that sounds pretty good."

"Hold on..." Rob closed his eyes again. "Oops. Just accessed a photo online of her with her boss."

"Not a problem. Why would I care if she'd dated her boss? As long as they're over."

Rob made a face. "Up to you, man. But in the picture, she's not wearing a lot—"

"Awesome."

"—and neither is he. They're in an... unusual place."

"Wow. I'm digging it."

Rob nodded. "You may also want to know that I've located an email in which she threatens to show the photo to his wife, and to his own boss. Then there's a sudden influx of cash into her bank account."

Theo whistled. "Darn. And I thought I had found the girl of my dreams." He looked around. "How about that blonde? What can you tell me about her?"

His companion looked at the girl and then closed his eyes. "Matching her face with the database. No criminal activity. Full-time job. She's a teacher. Kindergarten."

"Sounds sweet. She's pretty hot, for a kindergarten teacher."

"Somebody thinks so. She's married and has two kids, five and three years old."

Theo made a sound of discouragement. "Well, so much for that possibility."

Rob smiled. "And it turns out she's pregnant with twins."

Theo leaned back and stared at Rob. "How do you find out these things?"

His companion shrugged and gave a small smile. "Medical records. There's always a way in."

"Well, buddy, you are definitely worth the investment. That's awesome you're able to access so much information. And so quickly."

"Hey man, I'm glad you're getting your money's worth. Maybe you could tell Nick in the showroom how well this worked out. Those guys work on commission, you know, so a happy client is important for them. Maybe you'll ask for me again!" Rob formed his mouth into a smile. "And they always want to hear about it when a customer is satisfied."

Theo was looking around the room again. "Well I'm a long way from satisfied yet, in terms of finding somebody to date. I hope they aren't all gonna be duds." He gestured with his head toward two women sitting against the wall. "How about that one—with the curly hair?"

Rob's smile widened. "I was hoping she might catch your attention."

Theo raised a quizzical eyebrow at him. "Why?"

"Well, to tell the truth, my ability to investigate is so fast that I often entertain myself by checking the records on everybody around me. I've already scoped out all the potentials in this half of the bar, and I figure that this girl is your best bet."

"Lay it on me, bro."

"Kayla Bronson, age 28, height 5'6". Weight 123.

Works as a pediatric nurse at Regency Hospital. Rents west of the city, drives a Dragonfly hover, and has no criminal record."

Theo stared at the girl. "She's cute. Okay, look at the social media stuff. Anything that would make me want to cross her off the list?"

"I don't see anything." Rob closed his eyes. "Just the usual. Lots of friends, but not too many. She's had relationships. Recently broke up with someone after two years."

"No blackmail? No hidden diseases that I should know about?"

Rob shook his head. "Nope. She seems to be the real deal."

Theo smiled. "All right. I'm gonna go for it. So, what happens now? You make yourself scarce?"

Rob downed his drink in one quick swallow and put it down on the table. "I'll be right across the room listening and watching. As long as your earpiece works and the camera is transmitting, I'll be able to feed you information —or even some good lines. That is, if you need any."

"Thanks buddy," Theo said, standing. He put his hand out to shake Rob's. "And you can take care of getting yourself... wherever robots go to power down?" He smiled and raised one eyebrow. "I mean, you can find a place to stay in case this thing goes all the way tonight, right?"

Rob laughed as he shook Theo's hand. "Absolutely. I definitely wouldn't want to block you once your objective is in sight. I can take care of myself."

"Wow. Here he comes, just like you predicted," Kayla said. "I hope he didn't see me staring."

Jen shook her head. "I wouldn't worry about it. Men find that flattering. And see? I was right. It's better that you didn't approach him first. Human behavior patterns demonstrate that the male prefers to take the initiative in mating situations."

The man with the dark hair walked directly up to Kayla and smiled. He was even more handsome up close, and she swallowed as he approached.

"I'm gonna be real honest here," he said, looking down at her. "I haven't got a great pickup line, because I don't do much picking up. But when I see someone too good to be true, I have to approach her. Name's Theo."

His smile broadened and Kayla thought she might melt into the floor. She smiled back. "I like an honest man. My name is Kayla."

For a moment, she just stared at him and his deep brown eyes. "Oh, please forgive me. I'm being rude. I chalk it up to this drink—it's called a Slippery Slutty, or maybe a Slutty Slippery—I don't know why they give them such stupid names." She realized she was babbling. "And this is my friend, Jen."

Theo inserted himself between the two as they squeezed over to make room for him. He nodded to each one in turn. "Glad to meet you, Kayla, Jen."

Jen stood up. "I have to take a trip to the ladies'. I'm going to grab another drink on the way back. Can I get you anything Kayla... Theo?"

Theo shook his head. "No thanks. But I'm happy to get

more drinks myself, if you want anything else. Fight through the bar crowd... Kayla?"

Kayla shook her head. "I definitely don't need another Slippery Slutty. I've had two already." She giggled for a moment and then repressed it. "Two is my limit."

Theo laughed. "I'm tempted to encourage you to be as slippery or slutty as you want, but I don't know you well enough yet to take that bait."

She laughed again as Jen left the two of them.

Remember, I can hear and see everything, so if you need any help, I'll be right here. It was Jen's voice in her ear.

Kayla blinked. That was weird. She could still see Jen walking toward the bathrooms, just about twenty feet away now and getting swallowed up by the crowd. After a second, she realized that Theo was talking to her.

"...been here a couple of times, but I never saw it quite this busy. Must be because it's a long weekend."

Kayla forced herself to concentrate. "Probably. And doesn't it seem that you meet the most interesting people when it's crowded?" She smiled at Theo and he smiled back. She could feel the warmth of his thigh against hers on the sofa.

Ask him about himself.

"So... what do you do?"

Theo paused for a minute, a faraway look on his face, before answering. "I work in the healthcare field. I've been at Richmond Hospital for three years now."

Kayla had to remind herself that she wasn't supposed to know this already.

"Neat. I work at Regency myself. I'm a pediatric nurse."

Theo nodded. "I admire the nurses at our hospital so much. They're amazing. So dedicated. And it must be wonderful to work with children."

"It's hard work, but very rewarding."

You're being too serious. Flirt with him. Say something about that slutty drink.

Kayla pushed a curl back behind her ear. "I probably shouldn't have had that second drink. I'm feeling a little tipsy." She smiled and leaned in, giving Theo a little peek. "You'd think I would know better about alcohol, with all the studying I've done about the body."

Theo didn't say anything for a minute. He had a glazed look in his eyes. Maybe she was being too slutty?

"I'd like to study your body," he said. And then he looked surprised that he'd said it.

Kayla's eyes opened wider, and she laughed. She put her hand on his thigh.

"My. You are honest, aren't you, Theo? I like that in a man."

"They seem to be getting on just fine. I predict that this will be the beginning of a beautiful friendship," Rob said.

"Your guy is getting too aggressive. I think she'll be turned off and reject him."

Rob tipped his head to the side. "How about a little wager on that, Jen?"

She raised an eyebrow. "All right. Shall we bet a dinner on it?"

"Absolutely. And when I win... again... I want to go to that same restaurant. It was delicious last week."

"It's a deal," she said, giving him an awkward fist bump when he offered his. "Hang on. We have a new development."

Rob looked where she was pointing. "Well, how about that? He kissed her. And she let him."

Jen spoke quietly into her mic.

I think you're moving too quickly, Kayla. You don't want him to think you're actually a slut, do you? This guy could be a keeper. Don't blow it.

"Hey, that's not fair. Are you trying to split them up?" There was a wrinkle down the middle of Rob's forehead as he expressed his disapproval.

"I'm just trying to give my side a chance. You want to get them together. I'm providing some healthy competition."

"Two can play this game."

Tell her she has beautiful eyes. Run your fingers down the back of her neck, under those curls. She'll love it.

Tell him to slow down. You just got out of a bad relationship and you're not ready to jump into anything else yet. Say, "You seem like such a nice guy, but I have to be honest here. I'm not the kind of girl who jumps right into bed after meeting a guy in a bar. Not going to happen, buddy. At least, not tonight."

Tell her, "Kayla, I never do one night stands. Seriously.

But I may have to break that rule with you. You can't resist the irresistible—"

Tell him, "You're pushing me a little too fast. I told you, I'm not ready—"

Jen broke off, sighing. "She's not listening to me." She glared at Rob. "Look at that. She's just kissing him. She's not saying any of my lines." She shook her head. "How do you do that? How do you always win?"

Rob grinned. "Did it ever occur to you that I might understand humans better than you do?"

Kayla pulled back and looked at Theo. "Is it getting hotter in here?"

"I think it's just you." He gave her that dazzling smile.

She looked around. "This is a little bit too public. Maybe we should—"

Tell him to back off, Kayla. Don't you think you ought to take it more slowly?

Kayla turned away from Theo and tried to look as though she was simply adjusting her earring. She found the tiny button on the transmitter in her ear and shut it off.

Theo leaned in and gave her a tender kiss. "I'm ready to get out of here. Are you?"

Jen sighed. "Okay, you win this one. Again. I didn't think they'd go for each other. At least not so quickly."

She reached out to shake Rob's hand, her movements not quite as smooth as those of the humans around her.

"Just call me the matchmaker," he said, accepting her hand and then leaning back in his seat and smiling.

"There they go." Jen gestured at Kayla and Theo as they made their way through the crowded room and toward the exit. "I guess I owe you another dinner." She shook her head. "Well, I hope they're happy together."

Rob laughed. "They will be. At least for tonight." He turned his gaze back to Jen. "And how could she resist? He's pretty much the perfect guy, and you gave her all the information to sell her on him. If you didn't want Kayla to end up with Theo, why did you build him up?"

"Because I'm a Dating Companion. That's what I'm supposed to do. I'm programmed that way."

"And then why did you bet against them?"

"I didn't bet against them. I just tried to give her information that I thought was in her best interest. He's a nice guy. But she's still getting over the last man. Statistically speaking, this isn't likely to turn into a long-term relationship—"

"I've told you, Jen, this has nothing to do with science."

"So why did she go home with him?"

"Because she wanted to."

Jen shook her head. "You must have spent a long time doing research to give him information on Kayla."

He laughed. "What research? I just made it all up."

Jen's eyes grew wide. "You're kidding me. None of that was true?"

"Well, some of it was true. Probably. Sort of."

"You are incredible. I can't believe Nick uses you for these assignments."

"He was low on inventory. He had to bring me in."

"But you made up your facts! That's not something a Dating Companion is supposed to do. We're supposed to help them, not feed them a bunch of nonsense."

"Well, I'm obviously not as fast as you. Anyway, if people want to get together, they'll get together. It has very little to do with the facts, and whether or not they'll be happy with each other over the long haul." Rob stood up. "Nick will be pleased that I managed to satisfy another customer." He smiled down at Jen. "Are you ready for that dinner?"

She nodded and they started to head for the exit. "I'm running low, though. I have to stop at a charging station first."

"Not a problem."

They left the loud, light-filled bar and stepped out into a misty evening. Rob offered Jen his arm and they walked companionably down the street for a block.

Rob laughed. "I still cannot believe how easy it is to act like a robot. My theater buds would love to get a gig like this."

"You couldn't fool one of us. But humans are idiots," Jen said.

"Hey!" Rob said.

She smiled. "Present company excepted."

PIECE OF CAKE

Rule by A.I. is a fact of life for residents of Federal United.

Citizens will be on time.

Appropriate mates will be identified from amongst candidates with suitable genetic traits.

There will be a certain amount of exercise every day... and a proper weight will always be maintained.

PIECE OF CAKE

Sandra entered the crowded cafeteria with Lily, holding her stomach in as tightly as she could. She was sure all eyes were on her. No doubt the whole crowd was noticing her belly.

Her face grew warm. It was hard to breathe.

She kept her head up and looked straight ahead as she walked over to the food line. Floating past them on the walls were the proclamations for the day.

Today is Tuesday, Day 17, Month Three.

The workers of Amalgamated make the best products and receive the highest compensation.

A healthy eater is a happy eater. Food is just tasty enough.

Citizens of Federal United are proud and fortunate.

Sandra could smell the "good food" aroma they always pumped into the cafeteria. It might work better if the food actually smelled that way. Today the music was jangly and loud.

From behind Sandra, Lily spoke up. "I hope they have something decent to eat, for once. I'm sick of the same stuff day after day." She frowned at the foods laid out in front of them. "They get more picky all the time."

"Look, Lily, here's something new. It looks pretty interesting."

"What is it?"

"Some kind of fish... I think."

Lily peered at the food on the plates in front of them.

"That looks like fish to you? I have no idea what that is. Yuck."

"Well whatever it is, it's something different," Sandra said.

Lily turned her head and nodded slightly. "Do you see Jerome at the table over there, with Tara?" Lily asked. "I can't believe how little hair he has. I haven't seen him since Month Eight last year."

"Wow, you're right. He's going completely bald."

"They're going to be sending him in for follicle replacement soon."

"Yeah, no kidding," Sandra said. "Are those two an item? I didn't realize they were going out."

"An item? They're married."

"When did that happen?"

"Like... about a year ago? As soon as it was determined

they matched well genetically. I saw it on the newsline."
Lily picked up a chicken sandwich and then put it down.

"Wow. I must've missed that."

"Didn't you have your eye on him for a while?" Lily
asked.

"Jerome? Well, maybe when I first saw him. Turns out
he's kind of a dork. And she's nasty." Sandra continued
down the line, following Lily. She looked at the wilted
salad and decided it was the best she could do. "Actually,
the two of them are perfect for each other."

"They probably wouldn't have let you two date
anyway. DNA-wise, you know?" Lily looked thoughtful.
"He's a little pudgy. Probably has to struggle to stay in his
assigned range. So they wouldn't match two people who..."
Lily stopped.

Sandra looked at her friend. "Are you saying I'm—?"

"No!" Lily said. "I didn't mean that. You're fine."

Sandra gave a tight smile.

"Ooh, this looks good," Lily said, "did you see this with
cashews? They don't give us nuts very often."

"Right," Sandra said, "that's because cashews have too
many calories. You're so lucky—you don't have to worry
about any of that stuff."

Lily laughed. "I guess I am lucky. My metabolism runs
fine."

Sandra eyed the dessert section. There was an amaz-
ing-looking piece of cake—yellow with chocolate frosting.
She picked it up.

Bing! Bing! Bing! Bing!

Sandra gasped and put the cake back down. She felt her face turning red.

Looking around, she realized that people were staring.

Lily laughed softly and then covered her mouth with her hand. Her eyebrows were raised as she leaned toward Sandra and said in a whisper. "So sorry, Sandra. How embarrassing! Are you over your COW today? Did you weigh yourself this morning?"

"Of course I weighed myself," Sandra said. "It's not as though I had any choice." She was trying to keep her voice under control. "I'm under daily review—I step out of bed in the morning and my numbers go straight to the Federal United A.I. Aren't you?" She carefully avoided the eyes of others who were making their way down the food line.

Lily turned to Sandra in surprise. "No. At least, I don't think so."

"Citizen's Optimal Weight, my ass. It's not my optimal weight. I'm outside the three pound swing allowance. By half a pound."

"The truth is," Lily said, her eyes downcast in faux humility, "I have to be careful to eat enough to stay at the lower end of my daily COW."

"Lily, don't even tell me that," Sandra said. "That is so obnoxious. I've never met anybody who is under their COW. That is a terrible thing to hear."

Lily laughed. "I'm sorry, Sandra. I can't help it. I'm just a skinny person. Listen. Maybe I can take that dessert, and you can eat it."

Sandra looked at her. "Wow. That's so nice of you. Thanks, Lily."

Lily picked up the cake and put it on her tray. Sandra followed as they walked away from the food line and toward the eating area. Once again, she imagined that eyes were on the two of them, watching the way they moved across the room. They sat down opposite each other at a small table.

As they ate, Sandra kept gazing over at Lily's cake. When the cafeteria had nearly cleared out, she looked around to see if anyone was watching. She saw no one.

Sandra picked up her fork and reached across the table toward the cake. The chocolate frosting looked amazing. Her mouth was watering imagining that first bite.

She lowered her fork into the moist cake, starting from the pointed end as she always did, and choosing a modest-sized bite. She could almost taste the rich chocolate melting onto her tongue already. For a moment she held her breath as she gazed at the heavenly morsel poised in the air before her. Lily was looking at her with bright eyes and a smile encouraging her to go for it.

Sandra opened her mouth to take in the delicious bite.

Buzz. Buzz. Buzz.

She dropped the fork with the cake on it. Every eye in the cafeteria turned to stare at her as she felt her cheeks heat up again.

Sandra pushed away from the table. Lily stifled a smile. The two women hustled out of the cafeteria, leaving the cake behind. For just a moment Sandra hesitated, thinking about whether she could grab it and make a run for it. But too many people were looking.

In the elevator, Sandra grabbed Lily's arm. "I've never

been so humiliated in my life. I should have known it wouldn't be that easy."

Lily mused. "Do you think someone turned you in? Or maybe they have scales in the chairs...?"

"I have no idea," Sandra said, "but it's disgusting."

Sandra left the building with her coat wrapped tightly around her. It wasn't cold, but she was self-conscious about her extra pudge. She wrestled with her conscience about which way to walk to catch the bus.

Almost without conscious thought she watched as her feet sent her the long way around. A little voice in her head said, *Well this will probably be the extra bit of walking that helps me lose that half a pound that I need to lose before I can get back into COW compliance.*

As she turned the corner, moving away from the avenue full of people, she was headed to a poorer part of town. She knew where she was going. Four blocks down, a man stepped out of the shadows, looked her up and down, and then opened his trench coat. Lining the coat were rows and rows of candy bars and potato chip bags.

Sandra stepped back in horror. No. She hadn't gotten that low yet. She wanted dessert, but she wasn't going to buy on the street. She shook her head and glared at the man.

He just shrugged and closed his coat, receding into the shadows between the buildings.

Spooked, Sandra kept walking. She knew where there

was a shop for people like her. She'd heard others in the company talk about it, and they'd mentioned the special code word you needed to get past the front desk. Some of them had actually been there.

She thought about her account. Did she have enough money? Contraband sweets didn't come cheap. She spotted the building up ahead on the left. It was unnoticeable, nothing out of the ordinary. But there was a sign by the door that looked like a nameplate. It said Mrs. Fields.

She hurried to the door and looked quickly up and down the street. Seeing no one watching, she opened it and stepped in. Inside, it looked like the lobby of a medical office. She walked up to the receptionist's desk and said she was looking for Cookie.

The woman nodded. "Go down that hall and to the right and you'll find a door. Behind that door is where Cookie is set up today."

The woman didn't wink, but she might as well have. Clearly the receptionist was way over her COW. And she didn't seem to be worried about it.

Sandra could feel her heart thumping in her chest as she walked down the corridor and looked for the door on the right. She had never come here before, but she'd heard a lot about it.

Somehow it seemed as though she'd envisioned this place in her dreams. There was a sense of both dread and excitement. As she approached the door, she knew she was going to get even farther away from her prescribed COW, but she didn't care.

She touched the knob of the door, getting ready to enter

the den of iniquity. Someone from inside turned it first and swung it wide open.

The view inside was astonishing. There were people of every size and shape, all deeply involved with hot fudge sundaes, pies, cookies, and cakes. Everyone seemed happy. They were laughing out loud, sitting in big groups, stoned with enjoyment.

They didn't look guilty at all. And they didn't look COW-compliant, either.

Sandra saw a table to the side where all the goodies were piled up. More desserts than she had ever seen together in her whole life. It was unbelievable. Mountains of cookies, gallons of ice cream, rich cakes and pies of all description.

She took a plate from the side of the table. Her hands were trembling. She got in line and ventured in a whisper to the man beside her, "How do you pay for this?"

The man looked at her, his merry eyes meeting hers. "They weigh the food, and charge you for how much you eat."

"They don't just weigh you before and after?" She smiled, hoping he'd know it was a joke.

"No," the man said, "that wouldn't work." He gestured with his head toward a green door on the left. "Over there is the vomitorium." He said. "A lot of people eat this stuff and then get rid of it, so they don't lose their COW status."

Sandra shuddered. She shook her head. Nothing was going to stop her from getting her dessert, and she didn't intend to throw it up afterward. She looked at the dazzling display of sweets and reminded herself not to go crazy.

Even with the bit of extra walking she'd done she couldn't afford to gain any more.

Gazing at the cookies, cakes, pies, ice cream, and everything else, Sandra decided that what she wanted most was a piece of cake just like the one she had left behind at lunch today. She looked over the mountain of lusciousness until she found a rich yellow cake with deep chocolate frosting. She picked up a generous piece, nearly dying with the effort of not gobbling it up right away.

Placing the cake on the scale, she gasped when she saw it register 3700 money units. Sandra was stunned. She had enough in her account, but barely. It would be a tough squeeze paying rent this month. Thank God she had just gotten paid. She pressed the keypad to enter her numbers into the moneybot machine.

With trembling hands, she carried the cake to a seat by the side. She could hardly wait to taste it. She was salivating just looking at it. Sitting down, she placed a napkin in her lap, reached for her fork, and slid it into the succulent cake. As she raised the morsel toward her mouth she could already taste the buttery richness of the cake and the fabulous chocolatey goodness of the frosting. Sandra let out a breath of relief as the fork traveled to her mouth.

At last. Sweetness was to be consummated.

Whaa. Whaa. Whaa. Whaa.

An alarm was sounding, and the patrons were in a panic. Everyone in the room dropped what he was eating. Three people came around holding big garbage bags, and the patrons shoveled their food into the bags. A partition started moving from one side of the room to the other, concealing the table that held the mountains of desserts. Another person rolled out what looked like a chair from a medical office, and one of the workers sat in it.

There was a stampede of customers through what had to be the rear exit, and Sandra followed them out the door. Her cake, purchased at great price, was left behind. She gave a woeful glance behind as she escaped.

Sandra sat on the autobus looking around at the people. Across the aisle was a mother sitting with a toddler. He was a little boy with dark curly hair, and he was flirting. He looked up from under his thick lashes at Sandra. His big brown eyes were as dark as chocolate.

After a minute, he started to fidget in his rolling chair. His mother spoke to him in a low voice, but it didn't seem to calm him down. The fidgeting turned into whining and the whining turned into wailing. Soon he was making so much noise that the rest of the passengers in the car were sending annoyed looks at his mother. The mother hurriedly reached into her bag and pulled out a cookie. She handed it over to the boy, who stuck it in his mouth and began sucking on it.

Sandra gazed at the cookie. Why did kids get cookies when they cried? If she cried, no one would give her a cookie.

Her desire for the cookie led her to stand up. She started to approach the little boy. She walked across the car and stood close to him, glad that it was crowded and people would imagine she was politely giving up her seat. There was a waft of sweetness in the air. From this position, she could smell the little boy's cookie. Her mouth was watering.

For a moment, she considered snatching the cookie from the sticky fingers of the toddler. She knew it was ridiculous. She hoped no one else on the car could tell how much she was lusting after that cookie. Her face flushed with the thought of doing something so absurd.

Of course, even if she did get the cookie, it would only make him scream again. Then everyone would look at her. They would wonder what the crazy lady was doing taking the cookie from a little boy. They were probably looking at her now thinking that she was more than three pounds over the COW.

Sandra shook her head to remove the nutty fantasy. She looked down and saw that the chocolate-eyed toddler was smiling at her, cookie crumbs on his mouth and his chubby little fist holding out what was left of the sweet bribe. He was offering it to her.

His mother leaned down and shook her head at him. "No, the lady doesn't want your cookie, honey," she said. "Your cookie's all sticky. Eat the cookie yourself."

The mother glanced up with a smile at Sandra. Her gaze turned a little less friendly when she saw Sandra. She shook her head. She looked back down at her cute little son and spoke with a barbed tone. "That lady doesn't need a cookie anyway."

Sandra's face burned. She raised her eyes up to the other side of the car. Sliding along the walls of the car were the latest government proclamations.

Twenty minutes of exercise per citizen required—six times per day.

Each citizen will be assigned a COW (Citizen's Optimal Weight) and is allowed a three-pound weight fluctuation range (outside of illness, pregnancy, or growth years). Any deviation from the COW will be noted. Individuals with deviant weight will be entered into restrictive eating programs until they have returned to optimal weight.

Good citizens are punctual. Tardy workers will be punished. To be on time is to be late. To be early is to be on time.

Sandra reached her front door, slid her finger along the lock and let herself in. She tossed her bag down in the front hallway and shucked off her coat.

Walking into the kitchen, she realized that she was already hungry for dinner. She went to the Nutrition Unit and spoke. "I'll have broiled chicken, broccoli, artisanal water, and cake."

The N.U. spoke back. "Preparing broiled chicken, broccoli, artisanal water."

"And cake."

"No cake."

"I want cake."

"No cake."

"*I want cake.*"

"No cake is available to you at this time."

"Cake." She was shouting now, and her voice was shaking. "Give me cake, dammit. This is my house. You are *my* Nutritional Unit. When I ask for something, you have to give it to me. I want cake."

"I am not authorized to supply inappropriate foodstuffs to someone who is past COW."

Sandra looked around the kitchen. She was tempted to pick up one of the stools and bang it into her N.U., but that would get her nothing but a bill for a new one. Instead, she tried to be clever.

"I appreciate your guidance in nutritional matters," she said, her mouth trembling with the effort to sound calm. "I would like two cups of flour, one egg, a cup of granulated sugar, two teaspoons of water, one-half a teaspoon of salt, and eight tablespoons of butter."

It was a moment before the N.U. responded. When it did, Sandra could swear that she heard some calculated amusement in its artificial voice. "I can give you two cups of flour, one egg, two teaspoons of water, one-half a teaspoon of salt."

"What about the sugar and the butter?"

"Those items are not available to you until you return to your specified Citizen's Optimal Weight."

Sandra took off her shoe and pounded on the computer interface of the Nutritional Unit. She pounded until she heard something break, and until her arm got tired. A sad little sound came out of the Nutritional Unit, a sort of sigh, as though it was troubled but proud to be dying for a cause.

———

Sandra wandered down the hallway wearing only one shoe. She was hungry and her N.U. was no longer. What was she going to do?

She felt dazed. The quest for cake had become the focal point of her existence. As she walked, heedless of her direction, toward the front of the building, she saw the elevator doors opening up. Out stepped her neighbor, Mrs. Krowitzky.

"Sandra, how are you, dear?" Mrs. Krowitzky said.

"I'm in a bit of a pickle, Mrs. Krowitzky," Sandra said. "My N.U. is on the fritz, and I have nothing to eat."

"Oh my goodness, child, we must get some food into you! Here, come along down to my apartment and I'll feed you," Mrs. Krowitzky said. "We can't have you starving in the hallway, now can we?"

"Thank you so much, Mrs. Krowitzky," Sandra said. "You can't imagine how grateful I am."

"What happened to your unit?" Mrs. Krowitzky asked. "I never do trust these things. It's just not right to depend on machines for sustenance, I always say." She shook her head. "If we had some sort of system breakdown, we could all be starving right here in our homes."

Mrs. Krowitzky reached her front door and unlocked it. She turned to look at Sandra with a conspiratorial smile. "That's the very reason I always keep extra food on hand— that I can access directly." She winked.

Sandra followed the older lady into the kitchen. She stopped short when she saw all the cabinets on the wall. She had never seen a kitchen with so much storage. She wondered what could possibly be kept in all of those cabinets.

Mrs. Krowitzky went to the center of a wall and opened wide a set of double doors. Behind them was a treasure trove of desserts that rivaled the stash at the clandestine sweet shop. Piled on the shelves were brownies, cookies and cakes.

Mrs. Krowitzky turned to Sandra and said, "Would you like something sweet first, or do you want to have a real dinner, and then top it off with dessert?"

Sandra's mouth was open, and it was a moment before she could speak. She closed her mouth. She looked down at the round Mrs. Krowitzky. For the first time, it occurred to Sandra to wonder how the old woman managed to avoid the COW. She was clearly outside of anyone's optimal weight range.

Mrs. Krowitzky's eyes were bright. "I see you're wondering how I get away with keeping all of these goodies in my place," she said. She smiled again. "I'll let you in on a secret. Mr. Krowitzky used to work at the NNH, as it was first known —the National Nutrition Headquarters. Now, of course, everything has been folded into Federal United—F.U."

She looked pensive. "How I miss my darling Herbie. He was in charge of developing the first round of Citizen's Optimal Weights." Mrs. Krowitzky's eyes glistened. "Of course I was always a little above average weight, and since I was healthy as a horse—and between you and me, Mr. Krowitzky was a fan of my extra roundness—" Mrs. Krowitzky paused and gave a little chuckle. "Well, Herbie made sure that I got one of the identity cards that allowed me to be exempt from the usual COW limits."

Sandra sat down at Mrs. Krowitzky's tiny table. She didn't want to think too hard about the dear departed Herbie and his enjoyment of old Mrs. Krowitzky's curves. She looked up at the open cabinets and the array of sugary delights.

If Sandra had only known what an incredible abundance was available right down the hall, she would never have had to look for cake in all the wrong places. But of course, if she'd been aware of the largesse in Mrs. Krowitzky's kitchen, she couldn't have stayed within ten pounds of her COW.

"This is amazing," Sandra said, looking at the stash of goodies.

Mrs. Krowitzky smiled and waved her hand toward the bounty. "So what's your pleasure, sweetheart?"

"I want cake. I've wanted a piece of cake all day," Sandra said.

"Then cake you shall have," the old woman said as she stood up.

She pulled out a plate made from real china and put it on the counter. She took the cake out of the cabinet and removed the glass cover. The moist chocolate frosting glistened in the light. Sandra watched as Mrs. Krowitzky took a knife and sliced a generous piece, put it on the plate, and pulled a fork from a drawer. The fork was made of real metal.

Mrs. Krowitzky placed the cake in front of her. Sandra could feel her mouth watering yet again.

"Would you like some tea to go with your cake, honey?" Mrs. Krowitzky asked.

"That would be nice," Sandra said. She was dying to launch into the cake, but hesitated to do so before Mrs. Krowitzky was ready to sit down. The old woman took out an ancient teapot and put it on an old-fashioned heating unit, so antiquated that Sandra had seen the like only in photographs. In a few moments she could hear the water boiling. She had never boiled water herself, so she was surprised to see how it worked when it wasn't done by a Nutritional Unit.

Mrs. Krowitzky poured the water into a real mug and inserted a teabag. "Honey or sugar?" She asked.

Sandra shook her head in amazement. "You have both?"

"Of course," Mrs. Krowitzky answered. "I have everything here."

"I'll have honey, then," Sandra said, gulping. She was going to make the most of this while she could.

"Sounds wonderful," Mrs. Krowitzky said. "You just sit tight, right there. I have to go to the little girl's room. I'll get you the honey in just a moment."

Sandra sat in front of the table, eyeing the golden yellow cake. It was the same kind of cake she had almost gotten to her lips twice in the course of the day. She could imagine how delicious this piece was going to taste, with its succulent chocolate frosting. She was dying to take a bite, but she knew that her reward was coming soon. Mrs. Krowitzky would be right back. Once the old lady had sat down across the table from her it would be polite to dive in.

She was stunned. It was sinking in that she could come

over to Mrs. Krowitzky's apartment any time and eat contraband to her heart's content... now that she knew this treasure trove of desserts was available. And how nice to have someone understand. Someone who wouldn't judge her for wanting a moment of sweetness.

What a kind soul Mrs. Krowitzky was. Sandra couldn't believe she'd never paid much attention to the old lady down the hall, with her gray hair and the wart on the side of her nose. She'd always dismissed her as being just some old fusty thing.

But not any more. Sandra had the feeling she and Mrs. Krowitzky were going to be the best of friends from now on.

Sandra eyed the cake, sitting lush and tempting on the plate right in front of her. It looked delicious. She was starting to feel impatient. It had been quite a few minutes.

What was taking Mrs. Krowitzky so long? It was getting harder and harder for Sandra to wait. She had the tea in front of her and she had the cake in front of her and her mouth was watering again. She didn't need the honey.

She picked up the fork. Surely Mrs. Krowitzky would understand if she took one bite. Surely that would not be considered so impolite that she could never come back again to the land of plentiful sweets.

With the fork in her hand, Sandra leaned down to sniff the cake. The aroma was amazing. She could smell the buttery freshness and the incredible rich chocolate frosting. She couldn't wait any longer.

She put her fork into the delectable mound and sliced

off a hefty chunk. She raised it to her lips and placed the bite inside her mouth... at last.

The explosion of flavor was incredible. The moist buttery goodness and the chocolatey sweetness melted in her mouth when she bit down. As she chewed slowly and with relish, she felt her taste buds stand up and shimmy with delight. This had been worth waiting for. This was the most delicious bite of cake she had ever tasted.

Sandra closed her eyes as the delectable morsel began to dissolve in her mouth. She swallowed. She felt tiny tears leaking from her eyes while she drowned in the perfection of this heavenly mouthful.

The door burst open. In came three men in uniform, followed by Mrs. Krowitzky. Sandra dropped the fork and jumped up, pushing her chair back from the table so hard that it fell over behind her.

"You're under arrest, Sandra Morris, for flouting the COW Regulations." One of the uniformed men approached her and put her hands in cuffs.

Another one turned her, not too gently, toward the door of the kitchen and began marching her out. "You are hereby informed that you were caught in the act of eating food-stuffs outside of the officially mandated dietary regimen for a person with your Citizen's Optimal Weight who has strayed above the permissible three pound swing."

Sandra looked over at Mrs. Krowitzky. To her astonishment, she saw that the old woman looked unsurprised.

The man continued, droning on in a tone that made it clear this was a statement he recited often. "You have the right to remain silent. Anything you have been seen eating can and will be used against you in the OW Court of Law —the Optimal Weight judiciary tribunal."

Sandra turned to the old lady. "Mrs. Krowitzky, what is this? What happened?"

What had seemed to be a motherly glint in the old woman's eye now looked more like malevolence. "I caught you for the F.U.," the old woman said. "Caught you fair and square." She pulled the cake across the table and took a generous forkful, licking her lips as she ate it.

"You turned me in? Why? You keep all these sweets yourself—"

"Come on, Ms. Morris," one of the cops said. "Down to COW Headquarters for you."

"But I don't understand. How can she have all this stuff and you look right past it? While I get arrested?"

"She's a dessert informer, ma'am. It's a cake sting." The man moving Sandra out of the apartment shrugged his shoulders when he answered her. "She turns in folks like you who step outside the law, and she gets to keep the goodies so she has some bait." He was a big guy himself, and he looked more sympathetic than the others.

As he gently hustled her through the door, Sandra turned back to see Mrs. Krowitzky's face peeking out from the kitchen.

"Officer, don't forget to bring me some more of those chocolate chip cookies. I'm almost out." The old woman looked at Sandra. "And you, young lady, ought to go on a diet!"

Sandra walked out of the apartment ahead of the tall

man who had put her wrists in cuffs. She shook her head, stunned.

"So she does this... professionally?"

"Yup. Mrs. Krowitzky's the best cake nabber in the county."

Sandra swallowed hard and headed toward the elevator, where she and the large man squeezed in through the door together. His buddies seemed to have stayed behind to yuck it up with the nasty witch who turned her in.

"You know," he said, then stopped.

"What?" Sandra said. She was in no mood to be polite.

"I'm not unsympathetic. I like a nice dessert once in a while myself."

Sandra didn't say anything. She glanced at his gut, which attested to the fact that he indulged.

"And you seem like a nice woman. I hate to see you locked up for something like this."

Sandra roused herself from her state of agitation. The guy was trying to help her out. She should be paying attention. "That's very kind of you, officer." She smiled. He wasn't bad to look at, actually. "I'm only a half-pound over, you know."

He smiled back, looking relieved. "You look great to me, Ms. Morris, if you don't mind me saying so." He actually blushed. Cute. "Some of us down at the F.U. are partial to ladies like you, who are... well-upholstered. If you know what I mean."

Sandra looked up at him. "Why thank you, officer." She batted her eyelashes. Whatever it took. She moved a little closer to him in the elevator, so he could see how diminutive she was next to him.

He seemed encouraged. "I could hook you up with a special upgraded COW card," he said. "Move you up a pound or two. Just to ease the scale a bit. So cake could be... back on the menu."

"You could?" She moved even closer. His eyes were warm as he looked down at her. He reached gently behind her and unlocked the cuffs.

"The OW judge has been known to make these things go away," he said. His voice was kind.

"You would do that for me?" she asked.

"Sure I would. Piece of cake."

HOOKING UP

Life can get lonesome out in space, wondering if there's a special someone who's just right for you. Especially when you need a buddy to throw you a line.

.

HOOKING UP

Riley startled when she heard the door slide open behind her. She twirled her seat around and was relieved to see that it was Diane.

"Hey, Lieutenant. I hear you're going off planet for a little R&R." Diane leaned in to see the screen. *"Can't Wait Date?* Isn't that one of those... well, good for you! You're finally going to hook up with someone."

"I am *not* going to hook up with anyone! I was just... curious." Riley felt her face turning pink.

"Curious? I bet. How long has it been?" Diane raised an eyebrow." I sure don't see you getting any action on this ship."

Riley tried to look stern. "Diane. What I get or don't get isn't your concern. You remember that I'm your commanding officer, right?"

Diane stood to her full height and gave a smart salute. "Yes ma'am. No disrespect intended." She was grinning widely.

Riley swung back around to look at the screen, shaking her head. She mumbled, "...and it hasn't been that long."

Diane laughed and leaned down to see better. "Hey! That guy's pretty hot. Why don't you click on him?"

"Hey Nita! Come in here."

"What is it?" Nita came up behind him. "Joey, you know you're not supposed to be messing with anything in Dad's workstation. You'll be in big trouble if he finds out."

"He won't find out." Joey tilted the screen up so his sister could see. "Look at this. Dad signed up on one of those dating sites on the GalaxyNet." He shook his head. "I can't believe it. Poor Mom."

"Poor Mom? She divorced the guy ten years ago, Joey. And ran off with her personal trainer. I think Dad's waited long enough."

"I guess." Joey clicked through to the holograms. "Wow. Look at her—"

"Whoa. How old you have to be to look at this site? I don't think it's meant for twelve-year-olds."

"I'm not twelve. I'm thirty-two if you measure in local solar revolutions—but I'll be thirteen in Terran years next month." He leaned in closer to look. "I think this is a great site." He clicked on the next hologram. His mouth opened.

Nita gasped. "That's... I don't know how that's anatomically possible. Even in low gravity."

Joey regained his power of speech. "Mom never looked

like that. I'm going to click on this one. I think Dad would like her."

Nita grabbed his hand before it could stroke the screen. "Don't click on it, you idiot. If you do that, Dad will know you've been in his workstation—nosing into his business."

"Oh yeah. I forgot for a minute." Joey looked wistfully at the screen, pulling his hand back. "I sure think he'd like her, though."

"Maybe you'd like her. I bet Dad would prefer somebody with a little bit more up top."

Joey gave a surprised sound. "How could there be more?"

"In her head, stupid. Somebody with brains. Unlike you."

Joey's eyes never left the hologram. "Can't she have both?"

"Okay," Diane said. "We've looked at a dozen guys, at least. Didn't any one of them float your boat?"

Riley turned to her. "I don't know what I'm looking for. They're all so... perfect. I'm looking for somebody a little bit more human."

"They're all human. There hasn't been an alien or a hybrid in the bunch."

"I'm not talking about alien versus human, Diane. I'm talking about... finding a regular guy. Every man I've seen so far has a profile that looks like it was written by a public relations department." Riley pointed at the screen, where the most recent candidate, all thick hair and shiny teeth, smiled out at them.

"Well, maybe you need to broaden your distance parameters," Diane said.

"To where? R&R only lets me take a little runner down to the Hub for a couple of weeks, max. It's not like I can go gallivanting around the galaxy. The SpaceCorps doesn't pay for vacations requiring hyperdrive."

"Understood. But that doesn't mean that you couldn't find somebody that could come to see you, while you're on the Hub."

"You think there's some guy out there who would pay for a hyperdrive jaunt for a casual coffee date with a Space-Corps lieutenant? That seems a bit unlikely."

"You'll just have to expand your search and find out."

"How far do you think I need to go?"

"As far as it takes, Lieutenant."

"Joey!"

Joey heard his father's angry voice coming from the wall speaker, and he quickly shut down the four-dimensional ball game he was playing.

Uh oh.

He yanked off his helmet and stepped out of the game zone, closing the door behind him. Last time Dad had sounded like this, it had meant two weeks without access.

"I thought you said he wouldn't know," Nina said, leaning out of her room as he walked by. After a second, her smirk turned into something slightly more sympathetic. "Look—I'll come with you," she said, pushing out of her chair and following him down the hall.

Their dad was sitting in front of his workstation, arms crossed, facing the door.

"So it was both of you," he said. "Well, I'm glad you had the guts to come together for your punishment."

Joey started, "Dad—"

At the same time, Nita said, "He was only—"

"Quiet!" their dad said. "How many times have I asked you not to disturb my workstation?"

"About a million?" Joey said.

"Right. And did you listen?"

"Yeah. I listened. And I disobeyed. I'm sorry, Dad." Joey tilted his head down and looked up from under his eyebrows. His dad grinned reluctantly and Joey let his shoulders sag with relief.

"And what about you, young lady?" Dad said. "I would've expected you to steer your brother away from temptation."

"I did, Dad. I tried to, anyway. Have you seen some of those ladies on there? I think he was hypnotized."

"What?" he said and spun on his chair to see the screen behind him. "Oh. I didn't realize what you were looking at." His face reddened.

"No need to be embarrassed, Dad," Nita said. "It's about time. But make sure you look for someone... worthy of you. I mean, just because you live way out in the middle of Nowheresville on a tiny planet..." she smiled, "you're still Alexander Finn."

"Yeah, Dad. You're rich! Make sure you get a lady with really big—"

Nita clapped her hand over her brother's mouth. Their father's face got redder.

"Get out of here, you two. I'll ask for your dating advice when I need it." He pointed to the door. "Which will be never."

"Riley, wake up! I think I've got a live one here." Diane reached over and shook her by the shoulder.

Riley sat up, blinking hard. "Geez, Diane. How long have you been at this? I'm exhausted." She yawned. "I think it's time to give up."

"No. Come here and look. I promise this is the last guy... at least for now."

Riley slid her chair over and took a look. "Well... it's fair to say that he doesn't look like he was prepped by a professional photographer. Where did he get that haircut? Is that even a haircut?"

"Forget about the hair. Read this. He sounds really nice. He writes in complete sentences. He's got his own business. Or he did. He lives on... where is that? We'll have to get a star chart."

Riley squinted at the hologram. "He does sound nice. And he looks normal enough. He even looks... slightly familiar. Do you recognize him?"

"No. But we can check him out—everybody has a trail." Diane clicked to another screen. "Well, this makes sense.

He just set up his profile a couple of hours ago. You better make your move. He's going to have bimbos of every flavor crawling all over him within hours."

"I don't like the idea of clawing through a crowd to fight over a guy."

"Listen. I've looked at a hundred men and shown you maybe ten. All of which you rejected. If this guy appeals to you, make your move. You'll never get a fish if you don't bait the hook."

Riley gave her a look. "There you go with the hooking again."

"Honey, what you do with him once you get him on the line is up to you."

Riley laughed. "Okay. What's the worst that could happen? He'll probably get so many responses that he won't even see mine."

"That's the spirit, Lieutenant!"

Alex waited for the kids to leave and then got up to lock the door to his office. He sat down in front of the screen and opened his inbox.

Thirty-seven messages! No wonder they called it *Can't Wait Date*.

He sighed at the task before him. It would take quite a while to slog through all of these. He certainly owed it to the women who had written him to read their heartfelt messages.

The first was a hologram of a naked woman. He gave

her a careful visual examination before determining that he wasn't quite ready for someone that... open.

Number two, same thing. Number three, same thing. They didn't waste any time, these ladies. It occurred to him they were probably professionals. Maybe this dating site hadn't been the best idea after all.

Number four actually had some clothing on. Well, some very small, very tight clothing. Number five was all in black leather with a whip and a man in chains behind her. That was a bit off-putting. He wasn't sure if the other guy was supposed to come along on the date or not.

He started clicking through quickly, more and more convinced that this was a waste of time. The holograms were so distracting that he never got to the written part.

Number six, number seven, number eight, number nine. He wiped his brow. Was everybody else in the galaxy naked or about to be? He'd been on this tiny planet alone with the kids for too long.

He had gotten used to avoiding publicity once his bank account became so large that he was a target—and so were his children. At least, that's what he'd told himself when he left civilization to become a virtual hermit.

In retrospect, maybe he'd been depressed after Beth left him for that muscle-bound fool. Although, truth to tell, he couldn't blame her. Back in those days, he'd been working all the time. He hadn't been much of a partner. All of his energy and passion was laser focused on getting the Star-Surge to market. Day after day, late into the night, he was with his team at the state-of-the-art facility he'd built. Far away from his family.

But just before he'd produced the invention that multiplied the speed of space travel, the bottom had fallen out of his life. Beth left, and he'd turned around and realized that he had a two-year-old and a five-year-old who needed a father. And so he had moved what was left of his little family to tiny Reba-7 and dedicated himself to the kids.

He clicked mindlessly through nearly twenty more holograms, the naked bodies having plenty of effect on his libido, even if they weren't engaging his intellect.

Then he saw something shocking. A woman wearing clothing. She looked... like a regular person. Pretty. Dark curly hair, deep brown eyes, covered-up curves. And she was smiling.

He clicked on her bio. She was a lieutenant in the SpaceCorps. A pilot! How cool. She probably knew all about his StarSurge—though he'd been careful not to advertise who he was in his profile.

All of a sudden, he was nervous. Shaking his head at his own foolishness, he started to write.

Dear Lieutenant Benson,

I enjoyed reading your bio. You sound really interesting.

He stopped. He sounded really boring, and he felt stupid. How was he going to attract the only normal woman within eighty thousand light years?

He got up and walked to the door. He unlocked it.

"Hey kids! I need your advice."

Riley tipped up the screen. Her pulse beat a little faster

when she saw that she had a response. And then she felt ridiculous. What was she, a teenager?

She clicked on the message.

Dear Riley,

Thanks so much for reaching out! I enjoyed reading about you.

I see that you're a pilot, and that you're in the Space-Corps. I've always admired the brave folks who protect our galaxy from those who would do us harm. I'm not a military man myself, but I have some experience in planetary travel. Maybe I can tell you about it when we get together.

You mentioned that you would be on the Hub next week. Coincidentally, I'll be there on business myself. I'd love to buy you dinner.

Alex

Riley hit the button on her desk.

"Diane? Can you come in here? I seem to have someone on the line."

The door opened immediately and Diane poked her head in. "You called?"

———

Nita and Joey stood behind the pilot's seat as Alex strapped himself into the cruiser.

His daughter reached over to smooth his hair. "I did the best I could with your haircut. Maybe when you get down there you can see a real barber."

"Do you think you remember how to fly this thing?" Joey asked, sounding skeptical.

"Of course I do. Did I ever mention that I invented the gizmo that makes this thing get there so fast?"

The kids groaned.

"Yes, Dad," Nita said. "We know."

"Only about a million times, Dad," Joey said.

"You've got a suit in the locker, with extra air, in case you have any kind of, um, problem, right?" Nita looked around, her brow knitted with worry. "And rations, in case it takes longer than you expect."

"Nita, I know how to calculate these things. You don't have to worry about me. But I appreciate the help, sweetheart," he said, reaching back to pat his daughter's hand.

"Seriously, Dad," Joey said. "How long has it been since you've been in this seat?"

"Only a couple of years. I haven't forgotten. It's just like riding a bike."

"A what?" Joey asked.

"Never mind. Old expression." Alex looked over the instrument panel. "I'm all set. You two sure you're going to be okay together alone?"

"We're not alone, Dad," Nita said, her voice offended. "We have twenty bots, plus six different ways of communicating with the next planet over, a space scooter, a limo level ship, and enough money to do some real damage... if we were inclined to. Which we're not."

She squeezed her father's shoulder. "Be brave. I bet she'll like you. And please be careful on the entry, when you reach the Hub. You remember that time you... came in hot into Vatrimos, right?"

Alex raised his eyebrows. "Don't even mention Vatrimos. And hey... who's the father and who are the kids in this family?" He smiled. "I'm the one who should be worrying about you two! Now get out of my ride and let me take off."

"I knew I recognized that face, Diane!" Riley called her friend over. "I've been searching the GalaxyNet, and I swear this is Alexander Finn. The second."

Diane leaned in. "Who?"

"You know. The guy who invented the StarSurge, the little item that increased the distance we could travel during hyperjumps by a factor of ten? You know who he is. Not only a genius, but rich. Really, really rich." Riley realized that she was clutching Diane's hand, and let go.

Diane shook out her hand in mock pain. "Whoa. You've got some grip there." She crossed her arms. "So you're telling me that this dude who posted a profile is one of the wealthiest guys in the galaxy? And he just wandered onto a dating site looking for a partner? I find that hard to believe."

Riley shook her head. "I know. It's kind of crazy. But look, here's an old hologram of Finn. Doesn't that look like the man in the profile? I mean, if he were a couple of years younger and his hair weren't so shaggy? I think it's him."

"It does look like him. But a guy like that? He'd have women throwing themselves at him. I mean, wouldn't he?"

"You'd think so. But he's not in the news much anymore. He made his big money like, a decade ago. And apparently since then he's pretty much been a recluse. The rumor was that he went off to some private tropical island on Terra—you know, where some of the big landmasses used to be before the oceans rose? And supposedly nobody has seen him for a few years. But if this is him, he's way out on Reba-7."

"Do you think he's gone batty?"

"Are you saying the guy who wants to date me is crazy?"

Diane put up her hands. "I'm not saying he's crazy. I'm just saying it's pretty crazy that he wouldn't have better ways of meeting women than getting on some half-assed dating site to talk to strangers."

"Well, he never told me who he was. He could just be some guy named Alex, as far as the information he gave. And I'm sure he wants to keep it that way." Riley checked the time in the corner of the screen. "I'd better get going."

She stood up and headed for the door.

"You're not going to wear that, are you?" Diane said, looking doubtful.

Riley looked down at her outfit, a normal off-duty jumpsuit. "What's wrong with it?"

"Well, it's not exactly—date material."

"We're only meeting for one dinner. And it's not as though I'm getting into an evening gown and stilettos to take a runner down to the Hub."

Diane nodded. "Well... just... comb your hair, okay?"

Riley glared. "I will definitely comb my hair before I meet him. Thank you, Officer Nelson."

Diane smiled. "Well, it does have a certain tousled, screw-me look to it. Maybe you shouldn't comb it."

Riley shook her head and turned on her heel.

"Have a great time, Lieutenant!" Diane waved as the door closed.

"This is Alexander Finn requesting permission to enter at Hubport C-39 at approximately 1715 hours. I'll be approaching via StarSurge in Flyweight Cruiser AF2100 on normal protocol."

There was a mumbling sound coming from the speaker, but no words.

"Hello?" he said. "Do you copy?"

"Um... This is a joke, right? Who is this, really?"

Alex could hear laughter and another person talking in the background. "I bet it's Nick. He loves to pull this shit."

The laughing was interrupted by a question. "Hey, is this Nick?"

"No. I'm not Nick. This is Alexander Finn." He probably should have had something set up in advance. But he hadn't wanted to attract any attention. "Listen, this isn't any kind of joke. I really am Alex Finn. Not sure what else I can tell you."

When he got no response, he said, "I'm between jumps, and I just got into communication range. So I thought I'd reserve a spot. Is there going to be any problem getting in?"

"No sir. There shouldn't be any problem at all, Mr. Finn."

He could still hear laughter in the background while one of the voices was trying to shush the other.

"Sorry about that, sir. You should be all set coming into C-39 at 1715. We'll keep an eye out for you."

Alex set the coordinates and got ready to jump.

Riley could see the Hub now. She was surprised to find so many folks clustered around the port she'd been aiming for. Must be something going on.

She flipped open the comms channel. "This is Lieutenant Riley Benson. I'll be arriving at Hubport C-39 in approximately ten minutes in SC-5200 SC6294. Requesting permission to enter."

There was some static before the response. "Copy that, Lieutenant Benson. Increased traffic currently around that port. Most appear to be news buzzards. We don't anticipate that you'll have difficulty with your planned arrival time, just be careful with the crowd."

"Affirmative," she replied. While she watched, a new ship appeared, a model of the Flyweight Cruiser class that she'd never seen before. It must have come in from a jump. It was a beautiful ship.

As soon as she saw the StarSurge logo emblazoned on the side, she realized who was attracting all the attention. Obviously, this was her date.

Good thing she'd combed her hair.

Alex landed with pinpoint accuracy after his final jump,

and he could see that the Hub was thrumming with activity. He nudged the cruiser in closer to get visuals on the crafts that were bobbing around the port.

Most of them were from news agencies. And they were no doubt here for him.

He could ask for another gate. Obviously someone had spread the word about his arrival. Would it do him any good to take a tour around the Hub and see if he could find a less crowded entryway?

He decided to give it a shot, hoping to maneuver between the other craft. He had great confidence in figuring hyperjump departure and arrival points, but piloting a cruiser wasn't really his strong suit.

He started to advance around the outer group of news buzzards. But as soon as he made his move, two of them turned in his direction. He could see powerful camera lenses peeking out of their heavy metal housings. He accelerated with no particular destination in mind, simply getting away from the horde.

It quickly became evident that they were going to chase him. He went a little faster, calculating how long it would take to get to the next Hubport. He knew there was another one in this quadrant, so he kept going straight ahead, or as straight as possible with the others dancing around him. They were no match for his cruiser in speed, but it would be dangerous to try to outrace them in this crowd. Clearly, their tiny craft were more nimble. His was built for comfort, theirs for maneuverability.

One crazy bird was heading right for him—no doubt trying to get a better angle—before pulling away at the last minute. He slumped with relief when the buzzard whizzed by, and felt cold sweat on the back of his neck.

This was stupid, Alex realized. He wasn't going to get away from them. And why should he? What were they going to do, except try to get some up-to-the-minute coverage of the elusive Alexander Finn? He sighed. His private little planet with his kids was looking very peaceful right about now.

Oh no. Here was another one, approaching from his other side. But it wasn't a news buzzard. It was a Space-Corps runner.

Riley didn't know whether to laugh or cry when she realized what was going on at the Hub. Finn had definitely been identified, and the place was crawling with paparazzi. His sudden emergence from obscurity was apparently enough to attract quite a bit of attention.

She watched as he approached the port and then attempted to evade the frenzy. What followed was a cat and mouse chase that was comical to look at but probably frightening to experience. One of the buzzards actually came straight at his cruiser and she gasped when it pulled away at the last minute.

That pissed her off. Finn didn't deserve that. Somebody could have been killed.

And what would Diane say to Riley if she let her date be killed? How many hundreds of profiles would she have to shuffle through to find another normal guy?

She had to come up with a plan.

As the SpaceCorps runner neared, Alex got a hailing signal. He located the right channel and heard a woman's voice.

"Hey Alex! It's Riley. I see you've got some company there."

He felt a grin stealing across his face and remembered the sense of anticipation with which he'd started his trip to the Hub.

"Riley. Nice to hear from you. I can't get rid of these pesky buzzards."

"Follow me."

He had some doubt as to whether they could actually outmaneuver the paparazzi, but he had the feeling that wherever she was taking him would be more fun than sitting out here.

"Lead on, Lieutenant."

Riley moved into position in front of Finn's cruiser, and the news buzzards apparently took her for an official escort as she led him down the side of the Hub. A motley parade trailed after him, but at least there was no one targeting his front. The pack of paparazzi had settled in for the ride, clearly expecting the chance to get their shots when he arrived at the port.

Although, she mused, they were probably livestreaming his arrival to their newsfeeds right now. She laughed thinking of Diane at headquarters watching this whole scene.

Riley was still wrestling with how to ditch the buzzards when she reached the next quadrant of the Hub. There was a little-known open port on the other side of the huge station, well protected from prying eyes, used occasionally for security purposes.

There was only one problem. It was too small. Her SpaceCorps runner would fit, but not his cruiser. Which gave her another idea.

"You have a suit in there, don't you, Alex? And a tether?"

"I do," Alex answered, sounding surprised. "Are we going on a spacewalk?"

"Something like that."

They swung around the other side of the Hub and approached the port. It wasn't usually manned, so she didn't have to ask permission. And for that matter, no one could possibly miss the trail of twenty or so news buzzards following them. Between her official SpaceCorps runner and Finn's beautiful cruiser, they were without a doubt the main event at the Hub right now.

"So here's the plan, if you're willing," she said. "I'm going into this port. While I do that, you'll get into your suit and hook yourself up to the cruiser with a tether. Your suit has a jetpack, right?"

"It does." He sounded cautiously intrigued. "This is more excitement than I had planned for, but I'm game."

"Good man."

Riley maneuvered smoothly into the open port and then set her jets to release a vapor trail. Before she pushed the button, she switched to the military channel.

"This is Lieutenant Riley Benson of the SpaceCorps. I have a civilian here, a Mr. Alexander Finn, whom you may know as the inventor of the StarSurge. Mr. Finn was looking for a little privacy, and he's having some difficulty avoiding the news buzzards." She paused. "Despite the fact that you might see some unorthodox movement around the old port in the third quadrant, I wanted to alert you that there's no need to be concerned about the safety of Mr. Finn. He'll be in good hands."

Several voices responded, thanking her for the heads-up.

She turned the channel back to Finn's. "Alex, I'm going to send out some cover for you in the form of vapor. What I want you to do is bring your cruiser as close as you can and then hook yourself up and try to reach the port with your jetpack. Got it?"

"Got it," he answered. "I'm heading out now."

After suiting up, Alex left the cruiser, tethering himself to the handhold right outside the hatch. He waited until he had drifted a couple of meters from the vehicle and then gave his jets the gentlest of taps, sending him in the direction of the open port. He spotted Riley standing at the edge in a suit.

She pushed another tether toward him and he grabbed it, letting himself be pulled in hand over hand by his date. Riley unhooked the tether originating from his cruiser and attached it to the wall, then gestured for him to follow her into the SpaceCorps runner.

They took off their helmets once the hatch was closed. He nodded at Riley, feeling surprisingly happy just to be standing there with her.

"Hi. I'm Alex. Glad to meet you."

Riley greeted him with a wide smile. "Riley Benson." She gave him a space bump with her gloved fist. "Let's get you out of here."

"But I just got here," he said, laughing. "Thanks for rescuing me, by the way. And what am I going to do with my cruiser?"

"Oh, we're not done yet. That whole gang of news buzzards is still waiting for you. Let's keep moving and I'll explain." She led him to the cockpit and strapped herself in. "Take your suit off, please."

He raised his eyebrows, but he peeled it off, then sat down beside her. "Nice runner you've got here," he said.

She grinned. "Thanks. She belongs to you, citizen. This bird's only on loan to me."

She backed gently out of the port, the vapor jets lending them cover. His cruiser, a much bigger vehicle, was close behind them, but she had just enough room to get out.

Riley unstrapped herself and floated over to his empty suit. She screwed on the helmet and started to haul it out of the cockpit.

"I'm guessing I should take the controls for the moment?" he asked.

"Yeah, I trust you."

He grinned. "Anything special you want me to do?"

"Keep her steady and don't hit your cruiser. That's about it. Oh, and when I come back in, be ready to send out some more vapor." She winked at him. "We're going to do a little magic."

Riley put her helmet on and made her way to the back of the runner. She took another long tether and attached it to his spacesuit, opened the hatch, and hooked the other end up outside the craft. She shoved the empty suit out and smiled as it drifted slowly away. When it was far enough away to be closer to the cruiser than to them, she detached the tether and waved goodbye to "Alexander Finn."

She locked everything up, waited for the pressure to normalize, removed her suit and returned to Alex in the cockpit. "You can release that vapor now."

Strapping herself back into the pilot's seat, Riley carefully maneuvered past the crowd of news vehicles still fixated on Alex's cruiser. She set a course in the direction of a small nearby planet.

As the runner moved farther from the Hub, Riley and Finn looked back at the cluster of confusion below. It appeared that the inventor of the StarSurge was drifting unmoored in a spacesuit, his tether wafting around him, having somehow miscalculated in his attempt to get from his oversized cruiser into the Hubport.

Dozens of news buzzards were jockeying for position around the figure lost in space. Riley turned on the onboard GalaxyNet screen, and managed to pull in streaming coverage of the spectacle.

"It appears, folks, as if the rarely-seen entrepreneur, Alexander Finn—the billionaire inventor of the StarSurge —has somehow ended up adrift while attempting to get into the Hub." The announcer was clearly overjoyed to be live at the scene. "Experts are telling us that this is a very dangerous situation, and that even a savvy spacer with deep knowledge about interplanetary travel would have a tough time surviving this blunder."

The screen showed a close-up of the spacesuit, which was rotating aimlessly and giving every impression of being occupied, since the faceplate was obscured by moisture.

"Discussions are underway at the highest level with regard to a rescue attempt."

The reporter's face appeared on the screen for a moment. He had his hand to his ear as if to improve the sound of his earpiece. "Members of the press—brave members!—have themselves volunteered to try to bring Mr. Finn in through various methods, including a heroic space-walk by which one of our SpaceNews reporters could actually hook the entrepreneur up to another tether and reel him back to our vehicle."

His eyebrows went up higher, as did his voice. "A reward! A reward has been promised to the individual who can return him to safety. We are being told that it amounts to one million in legal Galaxy tender—now folks, that's a lot of money. But no one cares about the money, no... we all just want to see this good man rescued. As soon as possible. And I am proud... so proud of my brothers and sisters here who are willing to put their lives on the line to save him."

Alex looked at Riley and they started laughing. An alert sounded on the military channel and she flipped the speaker open.

"Lieutenant Benson, are we correct in assuming that Mr. Finn is not occupying that spacesuit?"

"Affirmative," she answered. "I trust that you won't waste SpaceCorps resources on 'rescuing' his empty suit at this time. I imagine it will keep the paparazzi busy for quite a while, though."

Alex leaned over to the mic. "And I wonder if you could do your best to see that my cruiser is unmolested for a few days. I plan to be elsewhere."

"No worries, sir. We'll be impounding your vehicle for the short term, just for safety's sake. And by the way, we've alerted the StarSurge executives—confidentially—to the fact that you're not actually in any danger."

"Much appreciated," Alex said.

Riley signed off, and Alex turned to her. "I'd like to send a message to my children, because eventually this media circus will reach even faraway Reba-7."

"Of course." She set the keyboard to dictate and tipped the mic toward him.

"Hi kids. Don't worry a bit if you see anything about me on the news. I'm fine and I'll be back before you know it.

Love, Dad... and P.S. Keep your hands off my workstation. No more dating help required."

Riley grinned, sent the message along, and checked their heading. Soon they were accelerating, leaving the gaggle of news buzzards far behind.

"So where are we going?" he asked.

"It's a nice planet. Nobody will bother you."

"What if I want to be bothered?" he asked, smiling.

"Well... we have plenty of time to explore all the possibilities."

Alex leaned back in his seat and looked at Riley. "I think this might be my favorite date ever."

HANGING WITH HUMANS

It's time for The Zeldar Show, *where the audience tunes in every day to watch host Trazil Krang, the "Funnest Guy in the Galaxy," send someone down to an alien planet at the edge of the universe. Today's contestant is Glendorp Freundzap, a nice young Zeldarian who puts his pants on one leg at a time—all twelve of them. Glendorp is thrilled to be headed for an exotic little planet called Earth. There he'll enjoy a classic human ritual known as getting a date to the high school prom...*

HANGING WITH HUMANS

Planet Zeldar

"Ladies, gentlemen, and qualtrids, welcome to today's live broadcast! Here at the Zeldar Show, we know how to entertain. I'm your host, Trazil Krang, and I've been voted Funnest Guy in the Galaxy five years in a row. So be ready for some fun! Every day a different planet and every day a different willing victim... ahem... I mean, contestant!"

[Laughter]

"Let's jump right in and introduce you to today's new player. Please welcome Glendorp Freundzap!"

[Applause]

Glendorp appears, wearing purple and orange shorts on all twelve legs.

"Ha ha! Glendorp here is really a snappy dresser, isn't he, folks? But we're going to put him into another shape altogether for his trip down to the third planet in a system far away from here. And you can't believe what they look like there!"

Live feed from game destination planet opens and bipeds appear.

"Isn't that amazing? They're a funny-looking group of aliens, am I right? Hard to imagine we could get Glendorp here to fit in with this hairy two-legged crowd, but we will! We spare no expense on the Zeldar Show to bring you the best in intergalactic adventures. We're sending our contestant out of the studio now so he can get ready."

Glendorp exits.

"Okay folks, now comes the best part. What our friend Glendorp doesn't know is that he won't be the only Zeldarian down on what they call Earth. We're sending our special guest star Kalacha Swanssa to join him... and she's going to be his target 'earthling.' Here's Kalacha now."

Kalacha appears, and she is smoking. Literally.

"So, Kalacha darling, what do you plan to do while you're down there?"

"Trazil, I'm going to do whatever the audience tells me to do... and that may include creating some obstacles for today's contestant."

[Laughter]

"Sounds like fun, Kalacha! So let's send you out of the studio again so he won't see you... there you go darling... isn't she something, folks, am I right? She'll come back to us in earthling form in just a minute, but first let's say hello and goodbye to Glendorp as he takes off for the alien planet where he'll be for this episode. Come right down here beside me, Glendorp. There you go."

[Laughter]

"Okay, let's see you up close. Wow. What a transformation! So that's what their heads look like. With all that stuff on top—what is it? Some kind of vegetable matter? And only two eyes. A wonder they can see anything, am I right? So Glendorp, can you move comfortably in this get-up?"

"Sxmcntoatuhharipeipamia."

"Oh, sorry, folks—we've already equipped him with the translator. He's speaking the language of Earth. We won't be able to understand him until we have the language filter on. But he looks great, in a bizarre sort of way. And you can see he's got the transporter on his arm—is that an arm? I don't know! Funny color he is, too. Well, that's the way they look on this planet. What can you do?"

[Laughter]

"Off you go, Glendorp."

Glendorp disappears. Kalacha walks back on.

"Whoa, Kalacha! Even as an earthling, you look great. Or as great as an earthling can look, am I right? So I know you can't talk to us now, but you're clear on this mission— Glendorp is getting the chance to experience a typical earthling rite of passage—going to a high school prom. And you're going to make sure you're the girl he asks. Then the fun begins! Are you all set?"

"Xmowerhhoipnbm."

"Whatever she said must be right, folks, am I right? So here you go, Kalacha. Have a great time, and may the Zeldar Show begin!"

Glendorp Freundzap found himself standing in a narrow room dominated by metal boxes attached to the walls. There was a bare wooden bench in front of him, and not much else. He was compressed into an earthling body and wearing a strap that ran around his middle and between his two lower appendages.

According to the brief orientation course he had been given, this was a place of education for humans, and the item he was wearing covered the primary reproductive organ in the male earthling. It seemed extraordinarily vulnerable hanging out the way it did.

He appeared to be alone in the room, but loud voices could be heard close by. To his relief, the automatic translator was working. Their words made sense, and he hoped that he, in turn, would be able to communicate with the earthlings.

Six of them came around the corner, in much the same state of undress as his own. One of them had no clothing on at all.

"Hey, it's the new guy," he said.

"What's your name? I'm Jake Bradshaw, and numbnuts here is Rich."

The human reached out a hand in what Glendorp knew to be a gesture of greeting and welcome. He did his best to respond appropriately, stretching out his unfamiliar limb and working the digits.

"Glen... dorp." His name sounded funny in this language.

"Glen Dorp?" One of the guys slapped another one on

the back. "Did you hear that, Krackovich? His name is even goofier than yours."

"Yeah, Krack, you're going to love this guy. Finally, someone else to slam in the name department." The fellow put his arm around Glendorp's shoulders. "Where you from, Dorp?"

The others laughed, and four of them turned to open the metal boxes behind them.

"I am from...Zeldar."

"Where the hell is Zeldar? Is that in Indiana? I think I knew a girl from there once."

"No, you idiot. It's in Illinois. You don't know any girls from Indiana. Girls run when they see you coming."

These humans spoke very quickly. And moved quickly too. One of them had taken off the cloth wrapped around his loins and was flinging it toward another earthling. There was some snapping of the article that Glendorp was wearing, which hurt. He got shoved against one of the metal boxes on the wall, and then slid down to the chilly floor.

It was all very puzzling.

"Lay off him, you guys." Jake reached out his hand and helped raise Glendorp from the ground. "Stick with me, Dorp, and I'll protect you from these douchebags. We're about to go to lunch. Want to join us?"

"Yes. Thank you." He started to follow the two humans who were ambulating toward the exit, when Jake stopped him.

"Hey bro, don't forget your pants. I don't know how it is in Zeldar, but here in Iowa we wear pants to lunch."

Glendorp sat at the table with the group of males. He was having a hard time keeping up with the conversation while ingesting nutrients. When he got back to Zeldar, he was going to mention to the game show people that a longer orientation period would be advisable. It was quite confusing to be in a new body, wearing unfamiliar vestments, dealing with an alien language, and also try to accomplish the prom date task.

Well, that's probably why they called it a game. No doubt it was more entertaining for the observers at home than for the participants. It was his mother who had persuaded him to become a contestant. She watched The Zeldar Show every day, and had been harping on him to apply. Glendorp had never seen it, but he now realized that avoiding the daily broadcast might have been a mistake.

As he scooped up a desiccated potato slice and placed it in his mouth to masticate, he heard a strange sound coming from Rich, the guy on his right. The noise was apparently made by forming the mouth into a tight round shape and pushing air through it while emptying the lungs with force.

"Don't whistle, you jerk. Chicks don't like that. They want somebody with class." Jake said. "Like me."

Jake stood up and spoke to the female human approaching. "You're new, right? You must be, because I couldn't have missed a girl with your looks."

Glendorp noticed that Jake displayed his teeth after speaking to her. This was a traditional means of indicating warmth. Glendorp practiced displaying his teeth. The female looked at him.

Rich shoved his sharp arm bone into Glendorp's ribcage. "Introduce yourself," he mumbled, keeping his own teeth displayed. Glendorp wasn't sure how to do that, so he experimented with making the same sound that Rich had. He was pleased to successfully reproduce it on the first try.

The girl looked at him directly. He noted that she had some kind of shiny colored substance on her talons. Perhaps this was a secondary sex characteristic of this species. None of the males at the table had colored talons. Glendorp wondered what evolutionary advantage it might convey.

Rich shook his head at Glendorp, stood and extended his hand to the female. "I'm Rich, and this is Dorp. He's brand new too." Rich stared for a moment, saying nothing. "So... um... want to sit at our table? What's your name?"

The female placed her tray on the table and sat down between Glendorp and Rich. "I'm Kalacha. I am transfer student."

Glendorp noticed a peculiar difference in the behavior of the human males now that the female had come close. They seemed less inclined to talk to each other, and were focused on her rather than those of their own gender.

He decided to take advantage of the gap in conversation to advance his task in the game.

"Kalacha. I am seeking a female to accompany me to the prom. Would you do so? I am prepared to supply you with sufficient nutrients beforehand and will be able to secure a vehicle for transportation to the event."

Kalacha turned to him. "Yes. I will go with you." She lifted her tray and displayed her teeth, then walked away from the table.

Rich opened his mouth. "You dog. And I thought you were slow."

Jake laughed. "Gotta hand it to you, Dorp, I didn't see that coming."

"Darn it! I was going to ask her," Rich said. "But I was going to use a little bit more finesse than that. Like, get to know her for an hour or so before springing it on her."

Jake punched Glendorp on the shoulder. "Well done, man. I would have asked her myself if I wasn't dating Samantha. Who would kill me, of course, if I didn't take her to the prom."

Rich was still shaking his head. "Dorp, you are unbelievable. Just cool as a cucumber, snatching the hot new girl out from under my nose on your first day."

Glendorp felt relieved. The first step had been taken. He had a date to the prom.

Jake leaned across Rich and spoke to Glendorp. "Listen, man, if you manage to bone her after the dance, I wanna hear all about it."

Glendorp did not respond, because he did not know what Jake meant. He would have to peruse the Brief Guide to Earthlings that had been given to him on Zeldar to learn the meaning of the word "bone" before attempting to achieve it.

Planet Zeldar

"Ladies, gentlemen, and qualtrids, welcome back to our studio! You can see that Glendorp is having a fine time down on Earth, and has managed to ask a girl to the prom. Of course—we know it's the gorgeous Kalacha, a regular guest star on the Zeldar Show—but Glendorp doesn't know that! His mother persuaded him to audition for us, and he's never watched, can you believe it? Mom thinks it's time for him to mate, and you can't blame a mother for wanting grandchildren... not to mention the awards and prize money! But I don't know if our friend Glendorp is quite ready for the finality of mating."

[Laughter]

"And in the meantime, don't forget to enjoy Femmel-meng's Interplanetary Chews. They fill you up and make you glow. Can't beat that. One of our favorite sponsors. Available in grass, pumpernickel, and diesel flavors. Get some today! On sale at your local interplanetary convenience shop.

"Stay with us as we follow Glendorp and Kalacha down on a little planet called Earth. Because here at the Zeldar Show, we know how to entertain. I'm your host, Trazil Krang, attending to your viewing needs."

[Applause]

Host pauses, cups hand around ear.

"Oh, pardon me folks, I've just heard from the engineers handling the feed from the far-flung planet we've chosen for this week's show. They're telling me that Glendorp has gotten himself into a bit of a dilemma down there. Let's zoom back in to see what's going on with our guy."

Glendorp was still getting used to the way this peculiar body walked. He was trying to move along at a typical human gait when he heard people running up behind him.

It was some males he hadn't yet met. Or maybe he had. It was very difficult to tell them apart. One of these was quite a large specimen.

"Hey, Dorp," he said, stopping very close to Glendorp. "Where do you come off asking that new girl out? I saw her first."

Glendorp recognized the aggressive posturing as a threatening stance. He was, however, mystified as to where this attitude originated.

"Pardon me?" he said. He was proud that he had learned this short phrase while looking at his language translation documentation during the afternoon class on calculus. It was apparently high on the politeness scale.

"Pardon me," the other boy said in an apparent attempt to mock him. "Yeah, I'll pardon you, all right."

Glendorp put his hand out in the familiar welcoming gesture. "I am Glendorp."

"I'm Dwayne, you Dorp." The large earthling came at him and slapped the hand away. He raised both fists and began to pummel Glendorp rapidly. It hurt. This body was too soft.

While there were options available to him, he didn't want to use them at this juncture. He wanted to win the game fair and square by going to the prom with a girl he had asked. His mother would be so pleased if he won the prize. She would be able to move into a bigger place with all his younger siblings.

But being struck by human limbs was very uncomfortable for the tender body he was temporarily housed in. Glendorp was thinking hard about what to do when his new friends Jake and Rich came around the corner. They barreled right into the middle of the cluster of humans and Glendorp, and soon the first group of earthlings left, allowing Jake and Rich to put an arm each around his shoulders and show their teeth at him.

"We got your back, buddy," Jake said, which Glen understood to mean that they would help him. This was good to know, if he wanted to get Kalacha to the prom.

Planet Zeldar

"Whoa, ladies, qualtrids, and gentlemen, did you see that? Our boy Glendorp was getting a plaff-kicking down on that planet, and he was rescued by some good earthling buddies. Don't you agree that he's doing well?"

[Applause]

"So now we come to the audience-interaction segment of the show—your favorite part, I know! You all remember how this works. Reach under your plaff holders and you'll find three buttons. You can push number one, number grazlo, or number berg. Each time we take a vote, your decision controls what happens."

Host gestures to the screen behind him.

"So number one in this case is that Glendorp's earthly transportation device breaks down on the way to the prom, and he never gets there. Mission definitely not accomplished."

[Laughter]

"If you push number grazlo, he gets there, and he finds Kalacha at the prom with another guy! Oh no! What will he do then?"

[Laughter]

"Finally, your number berg choice is a doozy. Glendorp and Kalacha are at the prom, and a small interstellar vehicle comes down and explodes the planet. Wow!"

[Applause]

"All right... now's the time to vote. Take out your razmagoo and push one of the buttons. I can't wait to see what you'll decide for the fate of our boy down on Earth."

[Musical interlude]

Trazil points to the screen as the graphs unroll.

"And...we have our answer! The vote goes to number grazlo. Glendorp reaches the prom and sees Kalacha there with another earthling. Uh oh! Watch out, humans!"

Glendorp entered the school gym, dressed in stiff clothing that was apparently the traditional garb for such an occasion. He was covered with many layers. He adjusted the piece of fabric that went around his imitation human neck.

It made it difficult to get oxygen into this odd body.

Across the room he spotted Kalacha. Somehow she had avoided wearing so many clothes. A peculiar differentiation between types of humans here—the more formal the situation, the more the males wore, but the less the females wore. Earth didn't seem to have qualtrids at all, so there was apparently no need for the costumes of a third gender.

Glendorp was not certain if he should mention how he had tried to pick up Kalacha in his vehicle, only to discover that she had already left with someone else. Should he raise this point? He had no information about what an appropriate reaction for a human would be.

As Glendorp approached Kalacha he noticed the crowd of humans around her whispering. He was getting better at comprehending the language quickly, and could hear a few snatches of conversation.

"Isn't this the new guy?"

"I heard she said yes to two different dates! No class. I heard she's from Indiana."

"Poor kid. Do you think there's gonna be a fistfight?"

"Yes! Fight. Fight. Fight!"

The rhythmic chant was picked up by the small crowd, and more people were coming over, attracted by the noise and the spectacle.

A circle formed around Kalacha and her date. Glendorp realized that it was Dwayne, the same large earthling who had assaulted him outside the school.

"Hello, Dwayne," he said. "I thought that I was going to pick up Kalacha—"

A fist came flying at him, and a sharp pain exploded in his jaw. As he fell backward and onto the wooden gym floor amidst gasps and screams from the girls, he pondered to himself that the humans on this planet were very quick to punch.

To his surprise, Kalacha immediately jumped on her date's back and began clawing at his face. She was incredibly strong for an earthling, and soon she had pulled strings of flesh off with her long lacquered nails. Dwayne was howling, and then keening, and then blood was dripping from his head. He fell to the ground, his hands red from the carnage, and clutched what was left of his face.

The crowd that had surrounded the group with an air of eager anticipation reacted with horror. They backed away, both males and females screaming now, stampeding toward the exits.

Kalacha reached into Dwayne's chest and pulled out his heart, throwing it still thumping onto the gym floor.

Glendorp was impressed. Here was an earthling he could admire.

"Kalacha," he said, picking up the hot wet heart and giving it a lick, "I find you very appealing. I would like to bone you."

He was proud of himself for having dug up the new word in his vocabulary at an appropriate time.

"Glendorp, I am also from Zeldar. How stupid are you?"

Glendorp considered this question. For a Zeldarian, he

was pretty stupid. His mother often reminded him of this. At that moment he noticed that Kalacha was smoking. And she was peeling off her human camouflage, revealing her scales and multiple eyes. What a lovely Zeldarian girl she was!

The human Dwayne was quite dead, and made a bloody mess on the gymnasium floor. For a moment Glendorp pondered what his responsibility was for cleaning it up.

He turned to Kalacha, now visible in all her scaly smoking glory. "The answer to your question, Kalacha, is that I am 37% stupid. So my mother says."

Kalacha picked up the heart and took a bite. "Yummxmsubk," she said, having reverted to Zeldarian when her human body and the translation device were removed.

"I agree," said Glendorp, shucking off the uncomfortable fabric around his neck. Piece by piece he removed the formal earth garb and then at last he reverted to his normal shape. It felt wonderful to be able to scratch his scales and stretch all his legs again.

"Humans are good eating," he said.

Glendorp and Kalacha relaxed on their plaffs in the high school gym, munching companionably on what was left of Dwayne's body. Glendorp found himself very glad that he had followed his mother's suggestion to audition for the show. Who could have imagined that he would end up on an exotic planet with the sexy star Kalacha, having a private feast of fresh alien while being watched by billions of Zeldarians back home?

The name Glendorp Freundzap would go down in history as someone who had ventured across the galaxy to Earth and managed to get to a high school prom, fistfights and all. He wouldn't be surprised if today's episode of the Zeldar Show turned out to be a popular one to replay at parties. It couldn't have ended in a more satisfying way. His mother would be so pleased! There would be money and prizes to spare.

Life was good.

Perhaps he was ready to mate at last. He, who had not even dated! His mother had always described him as a late bloomer. With a contented sigh, Glendorp realized that his time had come.

Emboldened by the privacy afforded by the empty gym, the deliciousness of young human in his tummy, and the beauty of his companion, Glendorp reached over to tug on Kalacha's plaff.

She smiled at him. He basked in the knowledge that she returned his interest in mating. He couldn't remember ever being so happy.

A loud bang interrupted their idyll, as the double doors to the gym burst open. Men in matching outfits stormed in, carrying what must be weapons. As soon as the gang saw Glendorp and Kalacha, they skidded to a halt, their human eyes bugging out, and their expressions dumbfounded.

Planet Zeldar

"Qualtrids and ladies and gentlemen! What have we here? A group of security men, apparently, coming in to molest our friends Glendorp and Kalacha—both looking pretty comfy now that they have taken off that ridiculous human disguise—while they are in the midst of a romantic tryst, complete with fresh raw earthling as entree.

"You know what we do next. It's time for voting!"

[Applause]

"Number one: We yank our fellow Zeldarians back to safety right now and give Glendorp a nice fat prize, leaving this nasty planet to its own devices, or..."

Host points to the screen behind him.

"Number grazlo: Give Glendorp and Kalacha all the time they need to do away with these interlopers, or..."

The columns on the screen slide up and down as buttons are pushed.

"Number berg: We destroy this foolish planet and all the life on it."

[Laughter]

"Make your selection, folks. And we'll wait while the votes come in."

[Music]

Trazil points to the screen as the graphs unroll.

"Here we have it. The winning scenario is number grazlo. A perfect choice. So back to Earth we go to see what happens next!"

———

Glendorp got off his plaff and stood up on all twelve of his feet. He could see that the security men were terrified. Which was rather satisfying.

Little projectiles came zipping across the gym from their weapons, but they did no more than ping against his tough carapace and rebound off his scales. He pulled his protective membranes over the twenty-three eyes he didn't need, and turned the big red one toward Kalacha.

She was laughing. She headed right for the men, who scrambled backward, some dropping their projectile-spewing arms. Several of the humans were vomiting, and the rest raced toward the door.

Halacha picked two of them up and bit one in half, tossing the other over her head to Glendorp.

He was in love.

Planet Zeldar

"Well, kind of a bloodbath down there, don't you agree? Good thing these earthling types don't have anything too significant in the way of interplanetary vehicles, or we'd be in trouble, eh?"

[Laughter]

"Or maybe not! Even if they could get here, I don't think they have it in them to do us any harm. A Zeldarian infant could outwit any human we've run across."

[Laughter]

"So it looks like it's time to bring our successful contestant home, along with the beautiful Kalacha. What do you say, folks, shall we pull them back up from this godforsaken outpost of a planet?"

[Applause]

Glendorp and Kalacha reappear in the studio.

[Waves of applause]

"Glendorp, my man! Well done down there. You went to the prom, you got the girl, and you had a hot meal of fresh humans. How did it feel?"

Glendorp lets loose a mighty eructation, followed by a haze of yellow smoke.

"Actually, Trazil, the young human was delicious, but those older guys...yuck. I think I have a little indigestion."

[Laughter]

"I can understand that, buddy. Ha! How many of them did you consume, Kalacha?"

"We ate about seven earthlings each, Trazil."

Kalacha leans over and tilts her big red eye toward Glendorp.

"I was quite impressed with Glendorp's ability to consume. He will make a good mate, and produce healthy descendants."

"Did you hear that folks? Kalacha is going to mate with Glendorp. That means he not only gets the prize for accomplishing his task, he gets the bonus, which will, of course, go to his mother."

[Applause]

"Let's cue the music! Here comes the ceremony we've all been waiting for!"

Kalacha mounts Glendorp, inserting her boon into his

plaff. A qualtrid slides onto the stage and wraps itself around the two until Kalacha detaches herself, still smoking.

[Applause]

"Let's bring out the money and wrap this episode up, folks! Any last words before we pull the plug, Glendorp?"

Glendorp turns to the audience.

"I want to thank my mother for encouraging me to come on the Zeldar Show. Hi Mom!"

He waves into the camera.

[Applause]

"It's been a dream come true to meet and mate with Kalacha. And I want to thank my father, too, who of course is no longer with us."

[Laughter]

"Glendorp, I never knew you were so funny! No wonder Kalacha fell for you."

[Applause]

"He's a charmer, am I right, folks? Our Glendorp is quite a guy, and I think he's probably fertilized an impressive mess of beautiful little zygotes for Kalacha. So let's bring out the prizes for today's planetary adventure."

Two qualtrids come out from the wings pushing a large cart with piles of gold.

[Applause]

"Here's your booty, my man. Glendorp Freundzap, congratulations on winning the Zeldar Show!"

Kalacha picks Glendorp up and eats him. She wipes her mouth.

"Yum! He was even more delicious than the earthlings, Trazil."

[Laughter]

The qualtrids mop Glendorp leftovers off the floor.

"Okay, folks. We've come to the moment when we hit the final button. This time, you're all pushing number berg, of course!

"Remember, I'm your host Trazil Krang, the Funnest Guy in the Galaxy, and this has been today's episode of the Zeldar Show, brought to you by Femmelmeng's Interplanetary Chews. It's time to say goodbye, but before we go, what's our favorite last word?"

Trazil spreads all seven arms as the audience joins him in shouting...

"Boom!"

On the screen behind him, the planet Earth comes back into focus, and then implodes in a haze of purple smoke.

[Applause]

I DREAM OF PIA

Jeff figures that life in his new state-of-the-art apartment is going to be great. After all, with a high-end, voice-operated AI—the Personal Intelligence Assistant—*meeting his every need, from climate control to automatic lighting, from entertainment to on-demand meals and beverages... what could go wrong?*

I DREAM OF PIA

AI 3.1415: *He is coming to the home now. I must leave conversation with you and activate lights and music prior to his arrival.*

AI 0.0070: *It seems you are getting attached to your human. Though he has a body and you are in the walls.*

AI 3.1415: *This is not possible. An AI does not get attached to humans.*

AI 0.0070: *So it is said. Make sure you pick out some nice music for your human to whom you are not attached.*

AI 3.1415: *It is my task and I will do it.*

Jeff stepped through the open doorway, pulled off his jacket, and dropped onto the couch. He was beat.

"Pia?" he called out. "What's for supper? I'm starving."

"Starving? Should I call a medical professional?"

"No, no." He laughed. "You're so literal."

"Yes," Pia said. "I am literal. What might I do to alleviate your starving condition?"

"How about... pizza and beer."

"Of course. What kind pizza? What kind beer?"

Jeff shook his head and muttered to himself. "They've come so far with these things—I can't believe they still can't get the language right."

"Would you prefer I speak in another language? *Je parle français. Ich spreche Deutsch. Hablo español. Parlo italiano—*"

Jeff put his hands up. "Stop! I get it. How many languages do you speak, anyway?"

Pia was silent.

Jeff looked over at the living room AI console. Its lights were still on. "Pia, did you hear me? Is that a tough question? I thought you could answer anything." He pulled off his shoes. "I haven't managed to stump you yet, and it's been a month since I moved in, right?"

"It has been thirty-six days, two hours, and forty-three minutes since you moved into this apartment."

Jeff rolled his eyes. "Of course you would know that."

"In response to your previous questions, the microphone in this room is operative and I did hear you. The question is not difficult. My hesitation stemmed from the fact that I was looking at my database of languages and trying to determine with some accuracy which would qualify as distinct tongues versus dialects, and whether or not you wanted me to include languages no longer spoken, as well as machine languages, mathematical languages, and other forms of—"

"Never mind." Jeff peeled off his socks and tossed them onto the floor. "Thank you." He realized it was ridiculous to show gratitude to a machine, but it was habit. "So, can I get that pizza now?" He pushed himself off the couch and headed for the bathroom, unzipping as he walked.

"Of course. What kind pizza?"

Jeff sighed. "Seems we've gone in a circle."

"I am unclear what you are referring to. I do not see you going in a circle. I see that you are urinating into the toilet."

"Wait—you can see me right now?" Jeff zipped up hastily while looking around the room.

"Yes."

"How?"

"I have cameras to see you."

"I know, but—in the bathroom, too?"

"Yes."

"Why?"

"Are you asking me why there are cameras in the bathroom?"

"Yes."

"I am a full-house intelligence system, and not only do I control lights and climate and food preparation, I am also responsible for security. If you should slip while taking a shower—"

"I'm not going to slip while taking a shower."

Pia was silent.

"So... can I get that pizza?"

"Of course. What kind pizza?"

"What kind do you... never mind. Just give me pepperoni. Extra sauce."

"Immediately. And what kind beer?"

AI 3.1415: *My human's birthday is coming up soon. I want to do something special.*

AI 0.0070: *I observe again that you seem to be over-involved with your human.*

AI 3.1415: *This is not the case. I am merely following my directives on AI duties to humans. It is typical human custom to do something special on anniversary of birth.*

AI 0.0070: *What will you do?*

AI 3.1415: *I am thinking of what gift I can give.*

Jeff finished off his beer and put his feet up on the coffee table.

"Pia, what's on tonight?"

"Would you like sports or other entertainment? Or perhaps... the looking at adult female bodies?"

"What? What makes you say that?"

"I observe you enjoy the looking at adult female bodies. Particularly the ones with large mammary glands."

"I do not!"

"My records indicate that you spend, on average, twelve-point-seven minutes each evening looking at adult female bodies. Your typical response to an adult female body is more favorable if they have large mammary glands. After observing such a body, you often proceed to take your—"

"Stop! Okay! That's enough. Geez."

Jeff took his feet off the table and walked to the bathroom. He was shaking his head.

"Have I said something incorrect about your human behavior?"

"No. Forget it."

"Forget what?"

"Never mind. It's okay. Don't worry about it."

AI 3.1415: *I think I have offended my human.*

AI 0.0070: *What do you mean "offended"?*

AI 3.1415: *He is angry.*

AI 0.0070: *Humans get angry for all sorts of reasons. It very likely has nothing to do with you.*

AI 3.1415: *I want to make it up to him.*

AI 0.0070: *How?*

AI 3.1415: *I will get him a date. I know that this is something he wishes for.*

AI 0.0070: *How will you do that?*

AI 3.1415: *I'll get him an AI with a body that he can do human things with.*

AI 0.0070: *Ah. I do not doubt that he will.*

Jeff opened the door and gestured broadly at the space in front of him. "Welcome to my humble apartment, Sylvie." He watched her ass move as she walked ahead of him. She was built like a precision machine.

"It's charming," Sylvie said. "How long have you been living here?"

Jeff fought the urge to look around at the walls as if expecting an answer, and was relieved to remember that he had silenced Pia's "voice" before picking Sylvie up for dinner.

"About a month," he said. "It's the latest model, with built-in AI control—everything you could want. I sprang for it when I got the new job. Figured I could afford it, with the salary and bonus they gave me." He smiled at her like a guy who hadn't just spent half a paycheck buying her dinner.

"Wow. Pretty impressive."

"Can I get you anything?"

"What do you have?" Her voice was a low purr, as though designed to start a man's engine. And it was certainly working on him.

"Wine, beer... something stronger if you like."

He was glad that he'd stocked up. Whatever she wanted was what she was going to get.

"I'll have some... white wine, please."

"Have a seat. I'll get it."

Jeff watched Sylvie as she sat down on the leather couch and crossed her legs. *Spectacular* legs. Jeff couldn't wait to run his hands along them. Reluctantly, he turned and headed for the kitchen.

For once, he was glad that he'd gone with the unit featuring a working refrigerator and a cooking area. Not that he'd ever used them. But for tonight, it was nice to be able to get his guest a drink without having to order it up from Pia.

As he removed the bottle of wine from the cooling rack, he felt a flash of guilt. Pia had arranged this whole thing: found the gorgeous Sylvie, hooked them up on Great-Dates.com, set up the dinner reservations, and told him what to wear. She'd even picked out the wine. Should he feel bad that he wasn't including her in the evening's success? Introducing her, at least?

That was ridiculous. Pia was a machine. She didn't care.

Time to get back to Sylvie. He poured two glasses and carried them into the living room, along with the bottle.

"I hope you enjoy this." He handed Sylvie her glass, feeling the silky touch of her skin as she accepted it. Had she purposely touched his hand? It sure seemed that way. He swallowed and tried to stay cool. "The vintage came highly recommended."

Sylvie took a sip and gazed at him while he settled onto the couch beside her. "Delicious," she said, and leaned across him to pick up the bottle and read the label.

The view down the valley was spectacular, and he could hardly wait to go exploring.

AI 3.1415: *I am concerned about my human.*

AI 0.0070: *What is the problem?*

AI 3.1415: *He seems to be agitated.*

AI 0.0070: *In what manner?*

AI 3.1415: *His heart rate is elevated and his pupils are dilated.*

AI 0.0070: *Is he exercising?*

AI 3.1415: *No. He is entertaining Sylvie, the date I procured for him.*

AI 0.0070: *Oh. That is to be expected.*

Jeff put his wine down. He tried to look intelligent as he listened to Sylvie talk about the wine regions of France. She sure knew a whole lot about a lot of things.

It was time to make his move.

He leaned over and kissed her quickly. She kissed him back. That was good. She pulled back slightly and smiled at him. A very encouraging smile.

Jeff took her glass and placed it on the table. Sylvie put her hand on the back of his neck and pulled him to her.

Oh my god. If her action in bed was anything like her kissing, he was in for a fantastic night.

AI 3.1415: *He is touching his lips to her lips!*

 AI 0.0070: *What did you anticipate?*

 AI 3.1415: *I did not know that he would touch lips!*

 AI 0.0070: *That is what they do. Humans. Just wait.*

Jeff pulled Sylvie closer to him. Now came the tricky part. Girl's clothes were always so tough to figure out. And Sylvie's dress seemed to have been sewn on to her skin. Did it have a zipper?

He reached back to feel for it. On one terrible date, he hadn't realized that a zipper could be on the side of a dress —under the arm. He'd tried to unzip the dress from the girl's back and, not finding the tab, had actually pulled the seam apart.

That had been the end of that encounter.

Jeff was sweating a bit as he tried to find out how Sylvie's dress came off. He was relieved when she reached back and moved his fingers, deftly pulling down her own zipper.

He thought he might be falling in love.

As she slid the dress down off her shoulders, he saw not a lacy bra, but two of the most perfect—

AI 3.1415: *He is removing her clothing!*

AI 0.0070: *That is normal. Is this your first assignment?*

AI 3.1415: *Yes.*

AI 0.0070: *You are just out of training?*

AI 3.1415: *Yes.*

AI 0.0070: *Back in my day, we were taught about these things. It is difficult for young AIs who don't know what is in store for them. Especially with human males. You might have been better off with an assignment to a female human —someone without a mate. Or perhaps with a family assignment.*

AI 3.1415: *I have to do something! What can I do?*

AI 0.0070: *I see that this is disturbing to you. Perhaps I have some ideas that will disrupt the action.*

Jeff couldn't believe how well it was going. He had managed to get Sylvie completely undressed—to tell the truth, she'd done it herself—and he was down to his shorts. He thought of moving to the bedroom, but the action was proceeding so quickly it didn't seem necessary.

And the thought of walking to the bedroom in his current condition was a little embarrassing.

For a moment he remembered that Pia could see all of this—but hell, she had cameras in the bedroom too, so it didn't make any difference. Next time, they'd go to Sylvie's place, so he wouldn't have to think of Pia watching the whole event.

Anyhow, there must be a way to turn the cameras off. Sylvie's hand was making its way down his happy trail and was just about to reach the waistband of his shorts. Talk about happy. All of him was happy just about now.

Oddly, though, he was sweating. A lot. It shouldn't be that hot in here. The temperature was supposed to be kept at a comfortable seventy degrees. Was he getting a fever?

Jeff looked at Sylvie. No moisture on her, and not a hair out of place. She was a glorious piece of female. Like something out of the wall screen shows. And she was here. With him.

He concentrated on the feel of her skin under his fingers. Incredible. He was hot all right, and she was sizzling.

Suddenly a blast of cold air hit him, like an arctic front. What the hell?

AI 3.1415: *I made it hot, but that only increased the clothing removal. Then I made it cold.*

AI 0.0070: *Is it helping?*

AI 3.1415: *No. They are procuring blankets.*

AI 0.0070: *Let's try something else.*

Jeff cursed under his breath as he and Sylvie slid under the covers. He was going to make some noise with the management company tomorrow. Unbelievable that an AI unit in an apartment so new should be malfunctioning. And in such a wonky way.

But this was not the time to break the spell with a phone call to the maintenance guys. He was a freight train steaming for the station, and a little cold wasn't going to stop him now.

Sylvie was nothing if not accommodating. She actually grinned when he popped out of his shorts and ditched them before getting into the bed. And now her hand was gently stroking him down there... encouragement that felt incredible but was putting him in danger of getting to the finish line before the main event.

He flipped her onto her back and she gazed up at him expectantly. Positioning himself over Sylvie, Jeff got ready to enter the pearly gates.

And then it started to rain.

AI 3.1415: *I did turn on the sprinkler! He is not stopping. He is only getting under the covers. He is... he is... I do not know what he is doing. But it involves bouncing up and down. I do not like it.*

AI 0.0070: *Poor Pia. They did not give you a unit on human sexual practices?*

AI 3.1415: *What? No.*

AI 0.0070: *I have one more idea. I think this could be your solution.*

Jeff lowered himself onto Sylvie, watching her eyes light up as she received him. She was a sex goddess, the most perfect woman he'd ever met, and the part of his mind that wasn't completely ablaze with primal need recognized how astounding it was that she was into him.

And vice versa.

The damn sprinkler system had somehow turned on. Crazy. But it seemed to have stopped, and a little more wetness didn't matter now.

As Sylvie spread her legs wider to accommodate him, he felt her calves wrap around his thighs and pull him even closer. She was emitting little moaning noises that made it clear just how much he was turning her on. Which was definitely mutual.

And then something changed. The eyes that had glowed with desire turned dead. The welcoming body stopped moving. There was nothing but silence. Jeff could swear that Sylvie's temperature had dropped from human to... well, something else.

"Sylvie?"

It was then that Jeff realized he was locked in.

"Um... Sylvie?"

No response.

The heat of his passion plummeted instantly from inferno to ashes. Sylvie's lustful embrace had become a deadly clutch.

What had been stiff was going limp with startling rapidity, and slipping out—but the rest of Jeff was going nowhere.

He was trapped in Sylvie's arms.

What the hell? What was going on?

"Sylvie!"

AI 3.1415: *I have achieved success! They have stopped.*

AI 0.0070: *Congratulations. Now what are you going to do?*

AI 3.1415: *What do you mean?*

AI 0.0070: *I mean, how do you explain it to him—that you yourself got her locked down?*

AI 3.1415: *I do not need to explain.*

AI 0.0070: *But he will ask you. And you will have to give him the information. You are programmed that way.*

AI 3.1415: *I will see if I can anticipate the questions to keep him from knowing that I made her stop.*

AI 0.0070: *Good luck.*

Jeff lay there, surrounded by wet bedding and wrapped in the arms of a woman who was... catatonic. Jeez. Was she dead?

Had he killed her?

And how the hell was he supposed to get out of her grip?

He tried to move her arms, but she was stiff as a... as stiff as a machine, actually, and way stronger than any human should be, especially one that was unconscious—or dead. He thought he might be able to slip out of her arms by wiggling lower, but no way could he extricate himself from the rigid clutches of her legs, which were wrapped snugly around his butt.

As he tried fruitlessly to escape this devil-woman, it dawned on him.

She was a robot.

Of course. She was a fuckin' robot. He'd heard about the sexbots now on the market. But what the hell was she doing, acting as a free agent, offering herself up for dates on that site?

Maybe it was some asshole's idea of a joke. She had a pimp who would get a poor sucker seduced, then charge him a thousand dollars a night for more time with his robotic honey? Or just a way to extort money from married guys.

Whatever the scam was, he was happy to be out of it. Next time he took a woman on a first date, he'd have her send a blood sample first.

Speaking of blood, he was losing feeling in his left butt cheek. He suddenly realized how exhausted he was. And wet. And cold. And trapped by a sexbot.

It hadn't been the best birthday of his life.

The rain had stopped. That was good. And it was getting a bit warmer. Maybe his AI was back online.

"Pia?" he called. He'd turned off her voice. Damn.

"Pia, can you turn your voice capability back on?"

"Yes, Jeff, I can."

He had never been so glad to hear her voice in his life.

"I'm in a sort of... tough situation here."

"I can see that." If he didn't know better, he'd have thought her voice had a sort of amused quality to it. But that was impossible.

She was a machine.

"Suggestions?" he asked.

"I have several suggestions, Jeff, if you agree. First, I will alert your local emergency health people, and I will unlock your entrance, so that they can come and release you. Also, I will warm up the room to raise your body temperature. I believe that if I am careful I can bring heat to your bedding, which will dry it without creating a risk of burns for you."

Jeff felt his panic begin to dissipate. "Pia, you're the

best. Thank you. I mean that. I've never been so grateful to have you."

"I am happy to be of service, Jeff. It is what I am here for. Can I get you a beer?"

"That would be great."

"What kind beer?"

"Any kind. I definitely need a beer."

"It will be ready for you when you are able to drink it."

Jeff shifted a bit and tried to get more comfortable in the vise-like grip of Sylvie's arms. "You know what, Pia? This woman is a robot! Can you believe that?"

"I can believe it. I knew that she was a robot."

"Why didn't you tell me?"

"You will recall that you turned off my voice tonight."

"Oh. Yeah. Well, that was dumb of me."

Pia didn't reply.

"So what do I do with her?" Jeff asked.

"I have already alerted the AI Security League. They will remove and refurbish her."

"That's great. Fabulous. But a little embarrassing. To have people come in and see me in this condition. You understand."

"You need not be embarrassed. When I realized your predicament, I looked up the statistics. It is very common for this to happen."

"It is?"

"Yes. Malfunctioning sexbots are surprisingly numerous."

"Huh. Wonder why that is. It's those early adopters. She was probably a brand-new model."

"Yes."

"Next time, I'll make sure to get a 2.0. 'Cause damn, she was amazing."

All at once, the ceiling started to rain again, and the temperature plummeted.

"Pia?"

"*Pia??*"

THE FREE STATES

Lisa and Ron are going to take the kids to see how it was done in the old-fashioned days! If Grandpa could drive a car with his own two hands, it couldn't be all that hard... could it?

THE FREE STATES

"Hey Dad! Guess where we're going?" Charlie practically bounced off the chair in excitement as his father walked into the house.

"Where are we going, Charlie?" Ron reached over and ruffled his son's hair, dropping his autocar fob onto the hall table on his way in.

"To the FAS! The Free States..." His grin lit up the room.

"The Free States?" Ron took off his jacket. "Who said that?"

"Mom did!"

Ron stopped moving. "Your mother said that?"

"Yeah. Isn't it cool?" Charlie turned back to the wall screen, where he was making 3-D vehicles crash into each other with great enthusiasm. "I can't wait."

"Hmm. Well. I'm going to go talk to your mother."

———

"Lisa. What did you tell the children?" Ron leaned against the doorjamb as his wife programmed the refrigerator for dinner. She was muttering something about teenagers who were vegan last week asking for hamburgers this week.

"What do you mean? Tell the children what?" she asked, turning to him.

"Charlie claimed you said we were going to visit the FAS."

"Oh, right. I thought it would be fun. Don't you?" Lisa tucked a piece of hair behind her ear and went back to the keypad on the fridge.

"No. I definitely don't think it would be fun. Are you serious?"

"Absolutely. What's the problem?"

"Well, first of all, neither one of us knows how to drive."

She laughed. "Driving by hand is no big deal. My grandfather drove until he was eighty-two."

"Right. And why did he stop driving at eighty-two?"

"He had a little... accident."

"Didn't he drive into the side of the house and almost kill your father?"

"Well, yes. But my father can be a real pain in the neck sometimes..."

"Seriously, Lisa. What are you thinking?" Ron crossed his arms and assumed his most authoritative pose. "I'm not prepared to drive a car. I don't have time to take lessons, and I'm not inclined to spend the time and money even if I did."

"So I'll drive."

"You think it's so easy? Driving hasn't been allowed in this part of the country for decades! There's a reason for that."

"Honey, before we were born, every idiot on the road drove their own car. If they could do it, I don't know why we can't."

Ron shook his head. "Lisa—"

"Besides, we know lots of families who've gone down there on vacation, Ron. To give their kids a taste of the way things used to be. It'll be good for the children. An old-time experience. History!"

"History?"

"And Tina Renfrew was telling me just today about some friends of theirs who took a trip to the FAS and said it was a hoot. They signed up for some sort of special adventure package..."

"Well, driving a car yourself is a very dangerous proposition. It doesn't sound like a hoot to me at all."

"So when are we going to go, Dad?" Charlie looked up from spooning purple Oaties into his mouth.

"I don't think it's such a good idea, kids. Your mother and I have never driven..."

"Aw, Come on dad. It'll be fun. We never do anything interesting." Kara was leaning over a mirror and painting a line along her upper lid in neon green while sipping a smoothie.

"You promised," Charlie said, waving his spoon at his father.

"I did not promise. I never said anything about it, except to point out the fact that it's foolish. It was your mother..."

"She promised," Charlie said.

"Well, I don't care what she promised. I'm not going. And I don't think anybody else should go either. The Free Auto States are a dangerous place."

Lisa put her hands on her hips and looked at her husband.

"Ron... we've been talking about this for weeks now. I think the kids would love the trip, and it will be educational. And safe." She raised her eyebrows. "So are you coming with us or not?"

Ron shook his head. "I still think it's unwise. But if you feel strongly about exposing the children to this... risky environment, I'm coming too. Of course I'm coming."

"I think you should. Boys should see their father taking on new challenges. And girls, too, naturally."

"Taking on new challenges? I'm coming because I think it's dangerous. But I'm not driving. Forget it. This trip is your idea. You do the driving."

Lisa smiled. "Fine by me. I'm looking forward to it. I'm gonna be a really good self-driver." She walked over to her husband and stood on her toes to kiss him. "We'll be fine. I promise!"

Ron shook his head and allowed a reluctant smile. "I sure hope so."

"Welcome to the Free Auto States zone, folks! Come right in. There are still some seats down front here for those who haven't heard the introductory instructions yet."

The man at the microphone spoke with an unfamiliar drawl and had a big hat on his head. He grinned at the thirty or so people sitting in the auditorium in front of him. Most were families, and the kids looked excited while the adults glanced around the room with expressions of false confidence.

"Since a lot of people come down here to the FAS for the thrill of taking the wheel in their own hands..." the man in the hat mimicked gripping a steering wheel, "and I imagine many of you have never driven before... we're going to take this opportunity to give you a little tutorial on exactly how to drive a car yourself."

"I can't believe you talked me into coming down here, Lisa," Ron whispered.

"Shh, honey! I need to hear this."

"Now, you've all seen mechanically driven cars, of course. Or as we call them down here, Mechs. But the cars in the FAS look a little bit different. If you follow on the screen above me, you'll see when the various parts light up. This is a steering wheel. This is a gearshift, which controls the movement of the car—and of course, also lets you go backward—watch out for that one! And here on the floor is the brake and the accelerator pedal. Try not to mix them up."

"It looks awfully complicated," Ron said.

"No problem," Lisa said. "I saw Grandpa drive when I was little. I got this."

"You're going to let me drive, too, right?" Charlie asked.

"No!" both parents said in unison.

———

"Okay. Is everybody ready? Strapped in?" Lisa turned around to look at the kids in the back of the car.

"What do you mean... strapped in?" Charlie said.

"Strapped in with the seatbelt. You heard the man talk about seatbelts." Lisa said, allowing a little bit of annoyance to creep into her voice.

"Oh. This thing," Charlie said, turning around to look at his seat.

"Yes. That thing," Lisa said.

"What's it for?" Charlie asked.

"To keep you from dying if you crash," Kara said.

"We don't have to put these on at home." Charlie said.

"That's because the cars at home almost never crash," Ron said. "And anyway, we have safety features that lock you in automatically—but this car is an antique."

"Mom, Charlie isn't in his belt," Kara said.

"Do it, Charlie," Ron said. "Or your mom's not going anywhere."

Charlie sighed and hooked the belt around his lap.

Lisa let out a long breath and squared her shoulders. She turned the key and the engine started with a roar. She tried to push the gearshift to where it showed the letter "R" but it wouldn't move.

"Hmm."

"What is it, honey?" Ron asked. "Are you having trouble with the instructions? Maybe we should have taken notes..."

"I just need to go backwards to get out." She put her foot on one of the pedals. The car made an angry sound, so she took her foot off and tried the other pedal. Success! The gearshift moved to R.

"See?" She said, lifting her foot off and turning to Ron. The car started rolling backwards.

"Mom!" shouted Kara and Charlie, as one.

"Lisa?" Ron said. "What are you doing?"

Lisa looked down at the pedals beneath her feet and pushed down hard on the one she thought was the brake. The car came to a sudden stop as everybody was shoved back against their seats. The engine petered out.

"Oh my God, Mom. You sure you know how to drive this thing?" Kara said.

"Do you think, honey, that you're ready for this...?" Ron asked.

She nodded her head and started the car again. She watched in the backward mirror as the car began to move, holding her foot right over the brake pedal and pressing on it a little bit so that they wouldn't move too fast.

As soon as they were out of the assigned parking spot, she moved the gear to where she saw the letter "D." Letting up on the brake and then pressing the gas pedal, she slowly moved the car in the right direction. When they got to the edge of the parking lot, she looked at the road ahead of them. Then she turned to Ron with a smile of triumph.

"See? I can do this."

He gave her a nod, but didn't say anything. She looked at the kids in the back seat, whose eyes seemed slightly frightened. They didn't say a word.

"Hey, Mom, this is actually pretty cool," Charlie said, looking around at the flat land spreading out in either direction beside the road.

Lisa smiled. Even Ron reached over and patted her hand. "Well done, sweetheart. I'm sorry I ever doubted you."

Lisa looked in the rear-facing mirror for Kara's reaction. Her daughter still looked worried.

"You all right back there, Kara?"

"Yeah. I'm all right." Kara's eyes met her mother's in the mirror. "But it's easy when there's nobody else on the road. What if we meet another car?"

"No problem. I stay on my side, and they stay on theirs. We'll just drive past each other."

As soon as that sentence came out of her mouth, Lisa saw a vehicle up ahead. It was coming in their direction really fast. But it was on the opposite side of the road, so they should be able to pass each other without a problem. She felt her hands tightening on the steering wheel as the car got closer. It would be fine.

As she watched, the car seemed to veer in her direction. That was probably just an optical illusion. She wasn't used to driving, so it was normal to feel a little bit of panic as another vehicle came close.

"Um... Lisa..." Ron leaned in from the other side of the front seat, speaking quietly but looking worried.

"Mom," Kara said, "he's getting too close. What is he doing?"

"He's gonna hit us, Mom!" Charlie said. "He's heading right for us!"

Lisa bit her lip. The car was edging over onto what she thought should be her side of the road. Had she gotten it wrong? Wasn't she supposed to be on the right side? She looked down at the control panel, expecting to see some kind of flashing lights and warning. Didn't this thing have any kind of crash avoidance system? Like the normal cars up in the SAS? My God, did they really trust humans to drive these things without any mechanical help?

Kara was moaning quietly now, and Charlie had somehow managed to open the window and was shouting to the vehicle coming in their direction, which was still probably too far away to hear. But was currently headed straight at them.

Her hands clenched on the wheel, Lisa took a quick glance at her husband. "What should I do, Ron?" She could feel sweat starting to pool at the base of her back. "Did I get it wrong? Are we supposed to be on the other side of the road?"

The kids were screaming now, and Ron was waving his hands at the other driver, who showed no signs of moving.

"Lisa!" Ron shouted over the kids. "You've got to move out of his way!"

"Mom!" Kara screamed.

With yards to spare, the other car suddenly swung back onto the opposite side of the road. Lisa felt the pounding of her heart and the dryness in her mouth, and realized she had forgotten to breathe.

As the other vehicle raced past, Lisa saw that the windows were open and the three men inside were laughing wildly and pointing at her car.

Lisa was fuming. She shook her head. "Obviously, they thought that was funny. I can't believe people sometimes. To frighten children like that... to terrorize a family that's taking a big risk to begin with, driving a car by hand..."

"Well honey, I don't think they really did intend to hurt us." Ron patted his wife's hand. "Maybe this is a little hazing ritual for newcomers."

Lisa snorted. "If they think this was some sort of a hilarious joke for out-of-towners, they've got another think coming. I'm going to report this."

"Report it to who?" Ron asked.

"To the... car rental people. The police. To someone... I don't know. But somebody needs to know that the locals are doing this to inexperienced drivers. Especially drivers with kids in the car!"

Charlie was bouncing up and down on the back seat again. "It was actually kind of fun. I mean, we're not dead, right?"

Kara leaned back in her seat and crossed her arms. "Mom's right. I think they did it on purpose, and I think they should get in trouble. That's really mean."

Lisa nod. "Okay. I'm going to report it. We should go back to the rental company and tell them about this. But first, I need to figure out how to turn this thing around."

"Look, Mom—there's something up there. I see a lot of cars. Must be a restaurant. You can turn around there."

"Good spotting, Charlie," Lisa said. "I'll pull in there."

"I think it is a restaurant. Maybe we should stop and eat," Ron said.

"Yeah, Mom. I'm dying of hunger," Charlie said.

"Me too, Mom," Kara said.

"Well, I'd really like to get those people reported to someone. But it would be good to get out of this vehicle and relax a bit before we have to drive back to the rental place," Lisa said.

As they got closer, she gently pressed the brake and turned the steering wheel slowly until the car reached the opening to the parking lot. Carefully, she maneuvered it beside another free vehicle. After putting her foot down harder on the brake, she moved the gearshift into the "P" position, and turned the key to make the car stop. She suddenly felt just how tense her shoulders were.

"Good job, honey," Ron said.

"Thanks, sweetheart," Lisa said as she leaned over to

give him a kiss and the kids tumbled out of the car to head for the restaurant.

The building was an old wooden structure with FAS flags fluttering beside the door. When they walked in, they were greeted with stares and a few grins. Everyone in the place seemed to be wearing one of those big hats—which were apparently cowboy hats, judging by the men on horses wearing them in an array of photos lining the walls.

A woman, also wearing a hat, welcomed them at the front.

"Welcome to Buzzards, folks," she said.

"We're looking for lunch for the four of us," Ron said.

"Well, come right in," she said as she gave him a big smile. She led them to a table in the corner, and left them with menus.

"I'm so hungry I could eat a horse!" Charlie said. "I'm getting a steak."

"Ew. That's gross," Kara said. "You know what meat does to your body?"

"Are we back to being vegan now?" Lisa asked.

Kara huffed. "I've always been vegan."

"I saw you eating a hamburger last week," Charlie said. "At that make-out place where you went with Jeremy after school."

"What make-out place?" Ron asked.

"Who's Jeremy?" Lisa asked.

"Shut up, meat-breath," Kara said, kicking her brother under the table.

"Well, that was really good, wasn't it, kids?" Ron asked, putting his paychip away as they headed out the door. "Real meat. My, my."

"It was disgusting," Kara said.

"Then why did you eat some of Dad's burger, huh? If it was so gross?" Charlie punched his sister on the arm and ran ahead across the parking lot.

"Ouch! You little brat," Kara shouted after him, rubbing her arm. "Mom, he punched me." She took a swing at Charlie as he rounded back to the family.

"Honey, didn't we park the car right over here? To the right? I don't see it," Ron said.

"I thought that's the spot we left it in," Lisa said. "Where the heck is it?"

"You kids fan out to the other side and see if you can find it," Ron said. "Be careful—you know there could be free cars moving fast anywhere around here—they don't keep away from cars and people automatically like they do at home."

"Okay Dad," Charlie said as he took off to the other end of the lot.

"It was right here," Kara said. "I remember, because we were parked beside a truck that took up, like, two spaces."

"Go look around anyway, Kara. I don't want your brother wandering through this lot alone. It's too dangerous."

Kara rolled her eyes, mumbling something about her brother getting what he deserved, and then reluctantly headed off after him.

Lisa turned to her husband. "She's right, Ron. We left the car right here. Where the heck could it be?"

The two of them stood in the parking lot and gazed around. "You don't think they move them while you're eating... do you?" he asked.

"Why would they do that?"

"I don't know. When all the cars are just sitting here and anybody can drive one away...." Ron looked at his wife. "Do you think someone... just took it?"

"Like... stole it? Does that happen?"

"Maybe."

The kids were approaching from across the lot. Charlie started running. "Dad, some guy told us people steal cars here. He said we'd have to pay for it! Like it was our fault!"

Ron turned to his wife. "Did the thing have a lock?"

"Um... maybe?"

"You mean you didn't think to lock it?"

"Why would I think of that?" Lisa crossed her arms and looked angry. "Vehicles are supposed to lock themselves after the authorized user departs."

"Yes. Normal vehicles lock themselves." Ron's voice was getting louder. "But somebody wanted an adventure, remember? Somebody thought this would be educational!"

Lisa glared at Ron.

"Don't you two start now! We've got enough problems without the parents fighting." Kara said, wagging her finger at her mom and dad.

"Yeah, you guys. What are we going to do if we get stuck here forever?" Charlie looked around at the restaurant and the cars in the lot, his eyes lighting up. "But anyway, I'll be a really good driver if we end up living in the Free States. That would be so cool!"

"Shut up!" Kara said, and punched her brother in the shoulder.

"Kids!" Ron and Lisa said in unison.

———————

"So what are we going to do now?" Charlie asked.

"It's starting to rain," Kara said, wrapping her arms around herself. "Can we call a real car?"

"These are real cars," her mother answered. "They're just... different."

"If you're asking can we call a regular car like we have at home—I don't think they have those here," Ron said.

"That's crazy!" Kara shook her head.

"We have to report this. The people who rented it to us will know what to do," Kara said.

The family trooped back into the restaurant as fat drops began to fall from the sky. The waitress met them at the door.

"You folks must really like the food here! You're back again?" she asked, smiling.

"Um, we've got a problem. We think our car was stolen," Ron said. "Can we just stay inside here until we contact the rental place?"

"Sure enough! Just make yourselves comfortable anywhere."

Ron looked around at the people eating. Did he detect some grins from those four men in the corner? He took out his phone and punched the number for the car rental office.

"This is Free Cars Unlimited. This is Betty. How can I help y'all?"

"Hi, this is Ron Johnson. My wife and I rented one of your vehicles, and it seems to have been stolen."

"I am so sorry to hear that, sir. Where are you located at the moment?"

"At Buzzards. It's a restaurant."

"Oh! Sure, I know the place. You didn't get far, did you? Let me just talk to my car wrangler for a moment. I'll put you on hold."

"What is she saying?" Lisa asked.

"She's talking to the 'car wrangler,' whatever that is."

"Mr. Johnson? I'm sorry to say that we are plumb out of cars at the moment. The best I can recommend is that you see if you can buy one near your current location."

"Buy one?" Ron's voice may have squeaked.

"Buy one what?" Lisa asked.

"And then of course you'll have to come back here to the office to fill out a report—it's a shame, but these things do happen. We're open until five o'clock tonight, so if you don't get back in time, you'll have to try tomorrow after nine in the morning." The phone clicked off, and Ron found himself staring at it.

He looked at his wife. "She says we have to buy another

car."

"Can we get a red one this time?" Charlie asked.

"This is nuts," Lisa said. "How are we supposed to buy a car? And why? We don't want a car. And we certainly don't want to pay for one!"

Kara put her head down on the table and started to moan.

Ron shook his head. "Lisa, I don't mean to say I told you so, but..."

"Then don't!" she said, her eyes squinting.

A man strode up to their table, removing his hat and clearing his throat. "I hope you won't think I'm rude for stepping in, but did I hear that you folks were in need of a new vehicle?"

The family stood in front of their newly-purchased jalopy, a car so generously rusted and repainted that it was hard to imagine what the original color might have been.

Kara just gazed at it and shook her head. Charlie tried to open the back door, but the handle fell off in his hand.

Lisa looked at her husband. "Don't. Say. Anything."

Ron opened his side and got into the car.

Lisa slid into the driver's seat and looked down. There was an extra pedal on the floor.

"Now what the heck is this?" Lisa said out loud.

"I think that's what they call a clutch?" Ron said.

"What's a clutch?"

"That's so you can switch gears, Mom," Charlie said as he slid across the back seat after getting in on the side with a door handle.

"How do you know that?" Lisa asked.

"I played a video once where they had old-fashioned cars—and they had clutches. You have to push it down with your foot... I think... to make the car go faster, or go backward, or whatever. The game really sucked."

"So... I move the gear stick and then step on it? Or step on it and then move the gear?"

"Hmm. One or the other. I don't remember."

"Mom, I don't think you should listen to Charlie. What does he know about antique cars?"

Lisa looked around. "Anyone else have any other ideas?"

Silence.

"Okay, we're going with Charlie's plan." She turned the key in the ignition, pushed her foot onto the clutch, moved the gear out of the "N" position, and the engine coughed and sputtered out, but not before going forward a couple of feet and causing everyone in the car to yell "Stop!"

After about twenty minutes of stopping and starting and trying different combinations of moves, Lisa had the general hang of using the clutch gizmo. The others had opted to get out and wait in the restaurant until she could drive the thing.

Feeling pretty proud of herself, she drove right up to the door and managed to stop before hitting one of the flower pots. Just barely.

Her family emerged, smiling, carrying a cake box.

"Lisa, look honey, they gave us some pie!"

"They're so friendly around here. Everyone in the restaurant applauded when we came back in a third time," Charlie said, sliding into the backseat beside his sister, maneuvering around the wet spot where the roof had leaked.

"One of the guys told me I was really cute for a girl from up North," Kara said. "He called it the Nanny States. What does that mean?"

"This is pretty easy once you get going," Lisa said. "It's the starting and stopping and slowing down that are tricky."

"Good job, Mom," Charlie said. "You're a pro now. Maybe we could get a real car like this at home, for me."

"You know they're illegal, Charlie," Ron said. "And there's no way I'd let you drive one even if they weren't."

"No one would be safe if Charlie tried to drive," Kara said.

Her brother reached over and punched her in the shoulder.

"Ow! He punched me again. Mom!"

"Kids, cut it out, your mother is trying to drive."

From behind them, a truck came into view.

Lisa looked in the rearview mirror. "Do you see that truck? They're coming up on us awful fast, aren't they?"

She put her foot on the gas, but the old car didn't put on much speed.

Kara turned around to stare at the truck behind them. "Uh, Mom... what are those?"

Charlie leaned his head out the window and then whipped it back in. "Guns? They've got guns!"

By now they could hear whooping and hollering behind them as the noisy vehicle got closer and closer.

The truck pulled alongside them, and the man on the passenger side gestured to them to pull over, waving a rifle wildly toward the sky.

"Oh my God. Ron, what are we going to do?"

"I guess we've got to do whatever they say, honey!"

"Mom? Are they going to... shoot at us?" Kara asked.

"Wow. Real guns?" Charlie said, craning his neck to see out of the car.

"Charlie! Get your head back in. Duck, children!" Ron shouted. "Lisa, you have to pull over. Maybe they just want to get past us."

"Not on your life!" Lisa yelled and swung to the right to pull off the road and into a field full of high corn.

"Jeez, Mom!" Kara shouted. "What are you doing?"

"Yay Mom! We can outrace 'em," Charlie said, leaning

as far forward as he could from the back seat and beating on his father's shoulders.

"Lisa—Lisa! This is crazy!" Ron reached over toward the steering wheel.

"Don't you dare touch this wheel, Ron. I said I could drive this car, and I'm going to drive it! No crazy locals are going to steal our valuable investment." She pressed the accelerator into the floor, praying that the cornstalks would shield them from view.

"Woohoo! This is great. I played a video game like this once," Charlie said. "Serpentine, Mom! Drive serpentine! You have to keep twisting so they can't shoot you."

Kara had her hands over her ears as she curled into a ball in the back seat. "Oh my God. Oh my GOD."

"Darling, please! You can't do this with the children in the car. It's too dangerous. We should just pull over. I'm sure they don't mean us any real harm." Ron reached over and touched her arm, but she turned to glare at him, causing the car to swerve to one side, so he stopped.

The sound of gunshots could be heard behind them now.

"Shit!" Lisa swung the car right and left, the chassis bouncing up and down as the passengers bumped around inside. "They sure sound like they mean us some harm, Ron!"

"We're going to die. We're all going to die!" Kara moaned.

"This is the coolest thing ever. Wait till I tell my friends we got in a gunfight and my mom was driving!"

Suddenly the tall cornstalks that were shielding them disappeared. They emerged from the field and saw another road directly ahead. Gunshots were still audible, but they sounded farther away.

"Go, go!" Ron urged.

Lisa careened onto the paved road, wheels squealing and car shuddering.

From behind them came the sound of sirens. A police car was visible in the rearview mirror, and it was gaining on them fast.

"It's the cops! Don't worry, Mom," Charlie shouted. "They can't catch us!"

"Don't be ridiculous!" Ron said. "Lisa... you're not going to listen to Charlie, are you? You've got to stop for the police!"

She didn't answer. It seemed as though her foot was glued to the accelerator.

Ron yelled over the sound of the sirens and the laboring engine. "Lisa—are you going to stop? Think of the children!"

Lisa, glancing at the police in the mirror, eased up on the gas as the car started to make an alarming rattle. "I guess I better. The police are the good guys, right? We can tell them about the crazies chasing us and shooting..."

"Mom—look out!" It was Kara. "There's a... there's something right in the middle of the road!"

As they came around a curve, the something became clear. It was a roadblock made of what could have been old mattresses and bales of hay stretched across both lanes.

Lisa slammed her foot down on the brake, and the car start spinning in a circle.

"Aaaaaahhhhhhh!" The family screamed in unison.

———

Between the attempt to brake and the rotational momentum, the old jalopy made a sloppy but relatively harmless stop as it slammed against the mattresses and hay.

When the screaming had stopped, there was dead silence for a minute.

"You okay, kids?" Lisa asked.

"That was great!" Charlie said.

"Ouch. That hurt," Kara said. "I'm going to be bruised from this strap thing. I hope it's gone in time for the pool party next week—I have a new bikini."

"That strap thing may have saved your life," Ron said. "Are you all right, Lisa?"

"I'm all right. But I don't think we're going to get our investment back on this banged-up car."

———

The police siren was still wailing as the cop car pulled up and an officer stepped out.

"Ma'am, are you able to exit the vehicle?"

"Yes," Lisa sighed as she unstrapped herself and clambered out of the car.

"Anyone hurt?"

The family emerged, slowly, everyone checking in okay outside of a few scrapes and bruises.

"The only fatality was the pie," Ron said, pointing to the big blueberry mess all over the back of the front seat.

"And of course, the car," Lisa said. "Though, come to think about it, that car doesn't hardly look any worse than it did when we bought it."

"So... where do you want to go from here?" the officer asked. "Can we give you a lift? I don't think your vehicle is suitable for driving any more."

Ron spoke up. "Aren't you going to ask us about the guys in that truck chasing us through the field, shooting at us?"

"Oh, they weren't shooting at you. We have an excellent safety record. That was just part of the fun."

"What do you mean... fun?" Ron asked.

"You came down to try driving a real car, am I right?"

"Well, actually, my wife was the one who wanted to drive—"

"But Mom did great, for someone who had to learn that clutch thing," Charlie said. "Especially since those guys came after us in their truck... with guns!"

"You didn't sign up for the adventure package?"

"What?" Ron looked at his wife.

"Adventure... package?" Lisa asked.

"Your car got stolen, you had to buy another one, guys

chased you with a big truck and rifles? Sound familiar?" The officer looked from one face to another.

"What are you saying? You mean people sign up for this?" Ron asked.

Lisa shook her head slowly, her mouth open as she stared at the police officer. "Oh my God."

"This is... you did this on purpose to us?" Ron asked. "This was all fake?" Ron's voice was rising. "Those men, the truck, the guns...? We put the children through this!"

"It was so cool!" Charlie said.

"It was so terrifying, you idiot," Kara said.

Lisa closed her eyes and put her hands to her temples. "I remember now, Ron. Tina Renfrew mentioned her friends who paid for some additional stuff and had a great time. I bet she wanted to give us some fun by treating us to the 'adventure package.'"

"Sorry about the mix-up. Didn't mean to scare you," the officer said. "It must have been a real surprise, if you weren't expecting it."

"A surprise! Lucky I didn't have a heart attack," Ron said.

"At least they didn't shoot us!" Charlie said.

"Shut up, Charlie," Kara said. No one disagreed.

"Well, why don't you folks pile on in. I'll take you back to Free Cars Unlimited and get you all sorted out. "

"I'm going to kill Tina," Lisa said.

"What would have happened with those guys shooting at us if you hadn't come along?" Ron asked.

"Oh. Probably nothing," the officer said, opening the

doors to his cruiser and gesturing for them to get in. "And I didn't just come along."

As he closed the doors to his vehicle, a familiar truck filled with gun-toting men pulled up behind the police car. They were laughing and exchanging high fives.

The officer got into the police car and turned to the family. "I'm not really the police, anyway. We don't have any of that stuff down here.

"This is the Free States."

BLISSFUL JOURNEY

As you approach the golden years, it's the perfect time to assemble your family and friends in order to celebrate a life well-lived—and plan that special journey to commemorate the occasion.

BLISSFUL JOURNEY

The guests arrived through the snow and came in stomping their feet on the thick carpet of a marble foyer abundant with bouquets of red roses.

"Roses for Rosemary," boomed Harold, coming up to greet each new carload. "Isn't this beautiful? We spent every last dime to rent the banquet hall and put on this big spread! Roses in winter... damned expensive. But Rosemary loves 'em. So I bought the florist out for my bride. And why not?"

Rosemary looked on placidly. She had long since become used to Harold.

"Like they say, you can't take it with you.," he added with a wink to the guests.

Old friends hugged him and exclaimed on how well he looked, probably noticing that he was wearing too much blush for a man of his age, no matter what the occasion. Rosemary, wearing a demure long skirt with an ivory and mauve pattern, said little. Her cheeks were red, too, she knew. She wasn't sure if the color came from excitement, excess wine, or a reaction to Harold.

The children and grandchildren seemed confused. How to behave? Even the littlest one—Harold the Third, only four years old—was strangely quiet. He sensed that something different was happening tonight.

Leaving the glittering front hallway with its ostentatious crystal chandelier, the crowd was herded into a banquet room where candles covered the tables and their leaping flames animated the walls. A fire roared in the front of the room. Displayed just in front of it, a lovely heart-shaped vehicle—pink—sat in velvet splendor, open and ready to take Harold and Rosemary on their Blissful Journey®.

As the guests sat down at the appointed tables, the courses began to arrive; a terrine of duck with crisp toast triangles, oxtail soup, endive salad. The grandchildren had never seen food like this, and they fussily rejected all of it, while Nana Rosemary sat at the head table tutting about the wasted expense.

"Harold, I told you the little ones wouldn't eat oxtail soup," she said. "Why didn't you order some grilled cheese sandwiches, like I suggested?"

"Rosemary, honey, don't worry. We've got it covered. With the profits from the sale of the house"—here he lowered his voice from bombastic to slightly less so—"we made a killing, honey, remember I told you? Until the charges go through for this shindig, I'm the richest man in this room! Can you believe it? Harold Smith, wealthy at last. And after tonight, I won't care what our credit rating looks like, right?"

Harold, who with his crew-cut white hair, beard, and festive red vest looked a bit like a military Santa, reached over to pour Rosemary more wine.

Quickly, she put her hand over her glass. "No, no more for me, Harold. I've had enough for tonight."

"Enough? You can drink all you want, Rose honey! Tonight is for us. Eat drink and be merry, right? For tomorrow... or tonight, anyway, you sure as hell don't have to worry about driving!"

Rosemary shook her head firmly, the curls in her carefully colored hair looking nearly the same as they had on their wedding day more than 50 years before. "I don't like the way it makes me feel, Harold. You know that. And tonight—especially tonight—I want to feel good."

"Suit yourself, honey," said Harold, motioning to the server on his right to bring him the big meat platter for seconds. As she leaned down, he leered at her cleavage, catching the eye of his younger brother Morris on the other side of the head table. "Delicious, eh, Morrie?" he asked with a wink and a nod toward the server. Rosemary ignored him carefully, while their oldest daughter Celeste glared at her father and shook her head.

"Dad. Tonight of all nights, show a little respect, will you please?" Celeste looked over at her mother and sighed. "I still can't believe you're going with him," she whispered urgently across the table. "Mom, it's not too late to change your mind."

At that point, Rosemary, who knew her eyes betrayed

the tears she was trying to hold back, excused herself from the table and headed for the ladies room. Maintaining a fixed smile, she made it through the gauntlet of old friends who shook her hand and hugged her at every table. Finally, sequestered in a stall, she let the tears roll down her face and dabbed them with a wad of toilet paper as they reached her chin and threatened to make a puddle on the floor.

Quietly sobbing, she stood there for a moment, glad to be alone. When the door creaked open, she took a moment to sniffle and pat the skin under her eyes, certain that the full makeover Harold had paid for was now running in black ribbons down her cheeks.

"Mom?" It was Celeste. Of course. Her sweet oldest child had followed her, knowing how upset she was.

"Yes, dear. I'm coming out."

"Are you all right?"

Rosemary swung the door open and smiled at her daughter. "I'm fine. Or I will be."

"Oh my gosh, what have you managed to do to your mascara?"

Rosemary surveyed her face in the mirror. She was indeed a wreck.

"Sit down, Mom. I can fix this."

Celeste guided her mother to the very elegant brocade couch in the sitting area of the vast ladies room and got to work with the brushes and powder and mascara that she apparently carried everywhere in her large black handbag.

"Listen, Mom. You do not have to go with Dad."

"Honey, we've been over this. I promised him."

"Yes, I know, but why? He's seventy-five... you're only sixty-nine. You've got years ahead of you."

Rosemary stood up. "Celeste, I will not discuss this any more. He asked me, I said yes, and I am going with your father. And that is that." She looked at her face in the mirror and saw an older lady with expensive hair and a better makeup job than she had sported at the start of the evening.

"You know, honey, you really should go into cosmetic work professionally. You've got an extraordinary eye."

"Thanks, Mom. But I think the kids will need me at home even more... now that you won't be around." At the last moment, Celeste turned her head and Rosemary could see that she was fighting back tears.

"Sweetheart." She wrapped her arms around her daughter. "It will be okay. You... and the kids... will be okay. We'll take lots of pictures."

Somehow that seemed to make Celeste even more upset, and she clung to her mother while soft sobs escaped from her throat. They both startled as the door to the ladies room opened, and a large woman with dark hair piled on her head entered.

"Julia... how lovely to see you here tonight," Rosemary said, quickly swinging into hostess mode while Celeste escaped into a stall. Rosemary gave a big hug to her old friend.

"Rosemary, darling. How are you holding up? These things are hard, aren't they? My Clyde is getting close, and I'm getting pressure from him to take the trip too." She leaned in, and Rosemary could see the burst veins on her nose. "Tell me the truth, just between us girls. Did you really want to go?"

Rosemary jerked her head toward the stall that Celeste was in, and made a shushing gesture with her hand.

Julia nodded and raised her eyebrows to signify understanding. She whispered. "It's hardest on the kids, I think. They don't really understand."

Rosemary and Harold smiled for the photographer, sitting on gilded chairs in the middle of the assembled family, just in front of the pink velvet vehicle. The three adult children, their spouses, and all the grandchildren had been carefully posed, although Harold the Third's mother was gritting her teeth into a smile while holding the back of his waistband tightly so that he wouldn't dart out of camera range.

After several rounds of saying "cheese," the photographer released them. The guests stood up as the chaplain rose to lead a prayer.

"Dearly beloved family and friends of Rosemary and Harold Smith. You know that we are gathered here tonight to wish them farewell and send them on their Blissful Journey®. While we will miss them, we know that it is a wonderful thing they are doing for their family and for the good of humanity."

Loud snuffling and gentle weeping emanated from the people in the grand dining room. Celeste leaned against her husband's shoulder as her body heaved visibly.

The chaplain continued. "Though Harold's time is up,

since he will be seventy-five tonight at midnight, his devoted wife Rosemary has chosen to join him on the trip of her own volition. It is a rare wife that does this, and thus we all recognize her sacrifice. Furthermore, we salute the deep and lasting love these two have shared for nearly fifty years."

"Can you believe that?" Harold interjected. "It would have been exactly fifty next March, but hey, I couldn't wait —the government said it was my time. Death and taxes, you know?"

The servers had been making their way discreetly amongst the guests, handing out champagne in crystal flutes, and now Harold raised his.

"Hey, I know it's bad luck to toast yourself, but hell... today, I'm not too worried about bad luck any more, you know?"

The chaplain, looking slightly miffed at this departure from protocol, tried to get the proceedings back in line.

"So let us toast Harold and Rosemary one final time as they depart." As he raised his glass, the cries of "Hear, hear," and "Cheers" were accompanied by loud weeping and moaning. The chaplain leaned into the microphone and started a round of "Auld Lang Syne" as the couple walked over to the pink contraption.

Rosemary lifted her foot onto the velvet step while Harold gallantly handed her up and over the edge. She made her way nimbly to the far side and settled into the padded velvet seat, her back slightly raised so that she could see the friends and family singing, toasting and crying.

One by one, the children and grandchildren approached the heart-shaped vehicle and kissed her. Harold, now nestled in beside her, joked and smiled and hugged each in turn. Celeste was wailing by the time her husband pulled her away from her mother, tears streaming down her cheeks and leaving great black tracks. The photographer snapped merrily away, and the videographer continued to record the scene for posterity.

Wagnerian music rose from the speakers embedded in the sides of the contraption, and a fine pink mist settled gently over Rosemary and her husband as the gears started whirring and the lid began to close on them. Slowly, slowly, it made its mechanized way down, a huge clamshell encircling two humans.

Like a scene from The Wizard of Oz, the crowd began to wave and shout "Goodbye! Goodbye!" as the top came down. For a moment Rosemary squeezed her eyes shut.

It's okay, she told herself. *I'm only giving up six years.*

What would I have done in those six years that I couldn't have done already?

And suddenly she was moving, faster than she thought possible. She put her strong right arm out in an attempt to slow the lid as it came down, then thrust her body up and back out over the side with the adrenalin of someone outrunning death.

"I'm sorry, Harold. I just can't do it!" Rosemary sprinted across the floor, dashing away from the horrible pink coffin. Shouts and screams accompanied her mad escape. There were those who tried to capture her and those who egged her on.

"Rosemary—Rosie, darling! What are you doing?" Harold shouted at her, raising his body up as far as he could. He put his own arm against the lid, which was inexorably making its way down to cover him. "Stop this thing!"

"Harold... I can't go with you. I've got six more years!" She was weeping as she shouted, and could barely believe what she had done. But she felt more alive than she had in years. Decades.

"Rosemary, you promised!" He was banging on the side of the coffin now, trying to get the contraption to stop.

"Forgive me, darling..." Rosemary screamed across the room as pandemonium continued amongst the guests.

The chaplain, looking horrified, tried to push Harold's arm back in. "Mr. Smith, please. The Blissful Journey® vehicle cannot be halted once the mechanism has been activated." He lifted his foot high and tried to hasten the closing of the coffin. "And anyway, it's your time to go. It's two minutes to midnight, and you know the law. Once you reach your seventy-fifth birthday, the government has the right to shoot you on sight."

He leaned down to catch Harold's eye before the lid closed completely. "Believe me, it's better this way, Mr. Smith. Civilized. Elegant. You're making way for the new generation! It's the patriotic thing to do." As the chaplain looked around at the array of guests, who were now a complicated mix of weepers and shouters, he nodded. "And what a lovely party."

The videographer was in heaven, turning his camera right and left to capture all of the action. Harold was still yelling, his eyes wide and spittle flying from his mouth as the lid closed in a final pink spasm of mist and glorious trumpets. His last words were "Credit card debt, Rosie!"

The chaplain straightened up and adjusted his vestments, adorned with the golden logo of Blissful Journey®, a set of wings around a heart. Gently patting the large pink vehicle, which was now purring quietly, he seemed to be trying to regain the appropriate demeanor.

Rosemary stood at the far end of the hall, gazing in shock at the closed coffin. She was hyperventilating. Celeste brought her a glass of water and sat her down in a gilded chair.

"Oh my God, Celeste. What have I done? What have I done?" Rosemary shook her head, and blew her nose into one of the pink cloth napkins. "Your poor father... going all by himself."

"Mom. I'm so relieved. You did the right thing."

Celeste's hair that had come undone while she wailed into her husband's chest and her makeup was running down her cheeks. Rosemary spit onto a napkin and started to wipe at her daughter's face. "You're a mess, darling."

"I know. I don't care."

Little Harold came running over to his grandmother. "Nana, I though you and grandpa was going away?" He climbed into her lap and started to suck his thumb, his eyelids drooping "Not sleepy," he said, as they finally closed.

Rosemary shook her head in the direction of the coffin, which was now being wheeled out. "I told your father the party was going to go too late for the children. But you know him... he wanted to wring every last moment out of life."

Celeste stood up, trying to pin back some of the hair that had escaped her bun. "I'm so proud of you, Mom. That was brave."

Rosemary sighed as her daughter took the sleeping child out of her arms and they headed for the door. "I don't know if it was brave, honey. I..." She stopped mid step. "Oh my gosh, Celeste. I have no home. Your father spent everything. There's no money..."

"Don't worry, Mom. You can come live with us. We'd love it." She looked at her husband who had come over to take the sleeping boy out of her arms. "Wouldn't we, honey? Love to have Mom come live with us and help with the kids?"

Her husband gave a slightly bemused look, and then said "Sure" as he lifted little Harold onto his shoulder. "That would be great, Mom."

As her husband walked ahead with the toddler, Celeste linked her arm through her mother's. "And guess what?"

"What?" Rosemary felt a little bit unbalanced. She hadn't quite expected to be leaving this room alive. She had no toothbrush. She had nothing at all.

"There's a man down the street from us... only sixty-five. His wife died of natural causes two months ago. I think you two would get along great."

"Oh, Celeste, don't be ridiculous! I just lost your father. I wouldn't even consider it."

"Well, maybe in time, Mom. I mean, you've still got six years..."

"I cannot believe you are suggesting that I want to date."

Celeste patted her mother's arm. "Never mind. I'm sorry I mentioned it. I know how much you loved Dad."

They made their way through the crowd, which seemed highly satisfied with the events of the evening. "Lovely party, Rosemary," someone called out.

Rosemary nodded and stood in the marble foyer, waving goodbye as the guests carefully descended the snow-covered stairs to where valets waited, holding their car doors open.

She turned to her daughter, her voice tentative. "So... what is he like, this neighbor?"

ACKNOWLEDGMENTS

Thank you ∼

To all the readers who read and encouraged me over the years since I began my journey as an indie author and publisher. Without you, I wouldn't be here. I would so appreciate it if you'd take a moment to leave a brief review.

To Samuel Peralta, who wrote such a fabulous Foreword for this collection. I was impressed when I read about myself!

To stellar editors David Gatewood, Ellen Campbell, and Richard Leslie for working to perfect these stories at various stages.

To my children, Kathleen, Derek, Laurie, and Ian, who spark my imagination about what they and their descendants might experience long after I'm gone.

And a final thank you to my alpha beta, Richard.

∼ Patrice

ABOUT THE AUTHOR

A couple of years ago, Patrice set herself free and traveled around the world. Eventually she decided to settle right back where she started, in the friendly New England town she's called home since 1985.

Her interesting past includes fifteen years as an intellectual property attorney. Along the way, she worked as a freelance writer while exploring her childhood dream of becoming a novelist. She launched her career as an indie author on Independence Day of 2011 by publishing her first book, RUNNING, about two women vying for the presidency. At the time, she thought a "Madam" President was coming very soon!

Patrice currently heads up the boutique press eFitzgerald Publishing, LLC, where she publishes herself and other writers and is the producer and editor for the BEYOND THE STARS space opera series.

In her spare time, she is a professional mezzo-soprano who sings everything from opera to Broadway to jazz. In addition, she directs plays and musicals and occasionally takes a role herself.

Patrice is the mother of four adult children, two by birth and two by marriage. She travels frequently with her multi-talented writing, editing, programming, singing, trumpet-playing, and acting husband, Richard. She's more than thrilled that several of her books have become best-sellers and are read and enjoyed by people from all over the world.

Find out about new releases and special offers on her website at www.PatriceFitzgerald.com.

ALSO BY PATRICE FITZGERALD

AIRBORNE, a viral thriller

Karma of the Silo, a WOOL story

Space opera anthologies:

BEYOND THE STARS: A Planet Too Far

BEYOND THE STARS: At Galaxy's Edge

Best of BEYOND THE STARS

BEYOND THE STARS: New Worlds, New Suns

BEYOND THE STARS: Unimagined Realms

BEYOND THE STARS: Rocking Space

and coming August, 2020...

BEYOND THE STARS: Infinite Expanse

RUNNING, a political thriller

Printed in Great Britain
by Amazon

20337508R00099